Richard Hayes
27.5.00.

SECRET DESTINATION

Tim Haughton

MINERVA PRESS
ATLANTA LONDON SYDNEY

ISBN 0 75410 652 7

First Published 1999 by
MINERVA PRESS
315–317 Regent Street
London W1R 7YB

Printed in Great Britain for Minerva Press

SECRET DESTINATION

To M and D

About the Author

Tim Haughton was born in Oldham, Lancs, and brought up in Stroud, Glos. After undergraduate and postgraduate study in London, he taught in Plzeň in the Czech Republic. Since returning to the green and pleasant land he has dabbled (with varying degrees of failure) in conference organising, tourism, book dealing and business intelligence. He even spent seven weeks in a Russian monastery. He is now safely ensconced in academia.

Part One

The Birthday Party

I LOVE BATHS. I love to wallow. I love to submerge myself in piping hot water. I love to lie there ensconced in my own little haven, my own little paradise. Perhaps in a previous life I was a hippopotamus. Hippos, however, do not wear their mother's shower cap, nor use a half-empty tube of toothpaste as a microphone. Their imaginations are not as fertile, but they do love to indulge themselves.

'Good evening, ladies and gentlemen. We're getting news that the Russian president has been shot. Over to our Moscow correspondent, Tom Reed.'

'Good evening, Tom.'

'Good evening, Jeremy.'

'What's the latest?'

I smile, clench my fists and exclaim, 'Yes!'

'Tom! Hurry up! It's ten thirty! They'll be here soon. We have so much to do.'

End of indulgence. My substitute microphone is returned to its rightful home next to the soap-holder. I reach for a towel, any towel, and begin to dry myself off. Dreams of headline news still flow through my mind.

Dad bought himself a new car last week. He didn't need a new one, but who was I to judge a man who thought that electric windows and an extra tenth of a litre were worth another two thousand pounds? At least it works. I allow Dad the honour of driving. Maybe I should be more assertive, but I have never seen the attraction of driving through cities, even suburbia. Traffic lights, kamikaze dispatch riders, and frenetic, blind, deaf and stupid pedestrians, unaware of the Green Cross Code, are not my idea of fun. Perhaps on a computer game, perhaps not. I'd prefer to display my masculinity in other ways.

Dad is a touch potty, but no one seems to mind. It is rather endearing. After arriving at the supermarket, we decide to split our tasks. I am to get the food, Dad the booze. Dad knows his wine, or at least he fancies himself as a wine buff. As I weigh the carrots, I can hear Dad musing aloud about the Chardonnay. His voice is just a little too loud to be classified as simply the mutterings of an eccentric; he *wants* to be heard.

A rotund woman pounding towards me shatters my mood of joy.

'Oh hello, Tom!'

The voice grates. Into those three words this mousy-haired creature packs all her contempt for me and my ilk. I don't want to enter into a conversation with her. She stands over me, replete with a pearl necklace. Her shopping trolley ostentatiously displays her taste. Her eyes have already scanned the contents of my trolley and concluded that the sun-dried tomatoes can't compensate for the own-brand baked beans.

'What are you doing now?'

A simple question, but seemingly simple questions invariably have far greater depth than the initially complex. Complex questions are precise, simple ones are vague. I know the pitfalls. Tell her all my successes (according to all objective criteria) and she would be upset. Sophie was my competition. She had probably just won the Nobel Prize, which would please her mother *so* much. Obfuscation is always the best tactic.

'I've just finished university.'

'Ah.'

I sense Mrs Smythe is tickled by my verb. I had deliberately avoided the verb graduate. She hopes I've flunked. She
wants to be sure. She wants to make me suffer.

'Finished? What', she pauses for emphasis, 'did you get?'

'A good mark.'

I am enjoying this.

'What mark?'

She snaps up my bait like a greedy warthog.

'I got… a…' I stumble in the manner of Hugh Grant,
not out of English bashfulness, but for effect.

'I got a first.'

'Oh!'

I do have a heart, so I decide not to ask how dear Sophie
was doing.

'Is… eh… that… the… time?' she asks rhetorically.
What a cliché! Still, I can't expect her to come up with
anything original. I feel great!

★

My earlier excitement has dissipated. I am beginning to
clock-watch. I periodically pick up the newspapers and
magazines from the coffee table, but after reading the
headlines, my concentration begins to wane. I feel so
anxious that I run upstairs and search for the invitation. I
check the date and the time. I wonder whether it really is
Saturday, 27th July, 1996. I run downstairs and look at
Dad's copy of the *Guardian* lying on the kitchen table. The
dates match. So why is nobody here? I'm beginning to
panic. Maybe nobody wants to come. Maybe nobody loves
me. I'm rescued from my paranoid musings by the doorbell. I rush to the door as quickly as I can and throw open
the door, a huge beaming smile across my face.

'Hello.'

I return the same greeting to this unexpected visitor. The dark suit and the black bag cause me to worry, Is this person who stands before me a long-lost relative or a Jehovah's Witness?

'I'm Fred.'

My mind is racing. Who the hell is Fred? My mind checks, University, no; school, no.

'I'm a friend of...'

Those are dreaded words for any host. Who, I wonder, has invited this chap?

'Of...' he is obviously nervous, 'Susi.'

Revelation! I realise instantly who this embarrassed creature is.

After expressing my sincere apologies for forgetting that Susi had asked whether her friend called Fred could come, I invite him in and try to kick off a conversation.

'So... eh... where have you come from?'

'Edinburgh.'

There is however no trace of Scottish accent in his voice. He realises the train of thought and quickly qualifies it by informing me that he studies there.

'I went there once, few years back. I drank a couple of pints of, what do they call it, *heavy.*'

'I... I don't drink,' he says with noticeable embarrassment.

My mind needs to race again. I stare up at the mantelpiece. A picture of my sister, hand in hand with her boyfriend on a French beach, stares back at me. Both are wearing swimming costumes, although Mick is wearing a pair of sweatbands. Football, that saving grace of conversation, should work.

'Have you been to see the footie at Hibernian or Hearts?'

'I... I... I... don't really like football,' he replies uncomfortably.

I refrain from asking him anything else about his adoptive city. Instead I pick an easy question. Simple and straightforward, I know, but I need to say something.

'So how was your journey?'

'Not too bad,' he replies rather curtly.

My sympathy for this guy, who wanted to come to my party, is rapidly waning. I know Susi has a soft spot for softly spoken souls who read poetry, but why does she have to invite them to my party? I'm not yet in the mood to enter into a conversation about Keats or Byron, so instead I ask the tritest question imaginable, how does he know Susi? The floodgates open. I have found his favourite topic of conversation. Although he waffles on and on and on, I feel more relaxed. He tells me in laborious detail how he had met her at an acting seminar in Leeds.

'She was impressed by my movement and my enunciation,' he tells me. He waves his hands around, clears his throat and continues to waffle.

Fred is obviously a character who is like a temperamental tape player. One presses play over and over again, fiddles around with the back, then tries every tape imaginable, but only when the greatest hits of Englebert Humperdinck is inserted does the machine actually work. Even though he's terrible, I console myself with the fact that it's better than nothing. Besides, I don't need to put in any effort; I can just sit back and relax.

*

The grandfather clock, which once belonged to one of Mum's long-lost relatives, chimes seven. I can only just hear it above the chatter. I glance around the room. Twenty souls are here. A few relatives, an odd assortment of schoolmates, but as of yet a mere two from university, three if you count Fred. Susi arrived an hour later to rescue me from Fred's eulogy on a theme of Susi. Fortunately, Susi doesn't talk about herself, at least not incessantly.

The doorbell summons me to the front door once more. I open the door and standing before me is a tall, blond-haired twenty-something, who is beaming at me through his Lennon specs.

'Hey, Tom!'

'Hey, Ed! Glad you could come.'

'Wouldn't miss it for the world. An evening of pure hedonistic delight,' he says while he raises his eyebrows in a suggestive manner. He reaches into his bag and takes out a package. 'Sorry about the wrapping paper, mate. Anyway, Happy Birthday and Well Done for getting a first. Git!'

'Thanks, mate. Come on in. What can I get you?'

'Anything.'

Clara arrives at eight. She apologises to Mum for being late, but she 'only returned from Paris four hours ago'. She looks tired. Her eyes display all the hallmarks of a hectic trip to Paris; the whites of her eyes have streaks of red running through them like raspberry ripple. She takes off her coat and sits down in the kitchen. She begins to relate a story about a rather adventurous night in Paris. I begin to drift off. My sister is not one of life's great raconteurs.

I grab another beer and one of Mum's quiches and move on through the French windows to a group of friends chatting at the end of the garden. Before I reach them, an all too familiar voice raises itself above the din.

'Tom! Over here!'

It is my dear Auntie Jane. She engages me in a long conversation on my future. I inform her of my new job starting in August and begin to outline my game plan. She is obviously proud of me. I feel sorry for her. Her children, my wonderful cousins, have not followed conventional paths. They aren't considered by respectable society to be successes. It is just fortunate that my dreams fit in well with society's expectations. I am a lucky soul.

Jane suddenly develops pangs of guilt that she is hogging me, the star attraction. She tells me to go forth and conjugate. I smile at her turn of phrase (even though she stole it from a film), wish her well and proceed on to Ed and Susi who are having an animated conversation with Fred. The subject is no doubt philosophical. Susi looks gorgeous in her tight-fitting, red summer dress. It displays all the reasons why so many men chase after her, but to win her heart one has to know one's Nietzsche, Shakespeare and Beckett. She has two admirers around her now, Fred, who travelled down from the Scottish capital, and Ed, who has confided in me his undying love for Susi. They are arguing, but far more interesting is their body language. Each stands with fingers pointing at each other, but with chests pointing in Susi's direction, displaying their intellectual prowess and their masculinity to the ultimate judge.

Susi notices me approaching. She calls out my name and the two combatants must halt their jousting. At that very moment they must hate me more than they hate the other. Susi starts to talk to me about my new job, a topic of conversation to which neither of the would-be Casanovas can contribute. They chip into the conversation, but their envy is clear for all to see, especially Ed, who had told me that he would try it on with Susi. I feel pangs of guilt, so I try to turn the conversation back to the original topic, but Susi, who is used to having everything her own way, refuses. I remember that we had got together once a couple of years ago, but it hadn't worked out. After a Saturday evening and Sunday morning of pure pleasure I had left her to go and watch a football match on the television. To her an afternoon of Liverpool versus Manchester United was akin to a visit to hell. She asked me whether this football match or our blossoming relationship was more important.

There is only one answer to that question, but as I sat in the pub four hours later, after a disastrous Liverpool defeat, I wondered whether I had made the right decision.

'There you are! I've been looking all over for you!' It is Clara.

'This is my sister, Clara.'

'Susi.'

'Hi.'

'Hi.'

'Fred.'

They both nodded.

'And of course you know Ed.'

Ed and my sister give each other a hug. After exchanging pleasantries, Ed hesitates and then asks, 'Is Mick coming?'

My sister hesitates, she gulps, she bites her bottom lip and then she mumbles, 'Yes.'

'Who's Mick?' says Fred.

'My boyfriend,' replies my sister.

Fred's disappointment is palpable. He thinks my sister and Ed may have had something on the cards.

Mick arrives at around ten. He greets me and gives me a present. Without further ado, I open it. It is a carton of wine. I thank him. He mutters something about it being nothing and then asks where Clara is. I point him in the right direction and return to my mingling. My mind however is racing again. Why was Clara so embarrassed and Ed so disappointed when she told him that Mick was coming? Why? My sister and Ed haven't seen each other for two years, at least to my knowledge, not since that journey through Europe. My inquisitive mind has been activated. I have to find out what is going on.

THE PUB, THAT centre of debate, discussion and poor chat up lines, is our meeting place. I arrive early. My lecturer was off sick with the flu today, so I had decided to stroll down Tottenham Court Road and Charing Cross Road to kill some time before I met Ed. In amongst the litter and the seedy shops stood foreign students with batches of leaflets imploring me to learn English. I resisted the temptation to inform them that my English wasn't too bad, thank you. It isn't their fault after all.

I am ten minutes early. I ponder whether I should go on in and sit alone or walk round the block again. I don't like sitting in the pub alone, I feel terribly conspicuous, with legions of eyes staring at me, telling me I have no friends. Ed likes sitting in the pub alone, a pint, a book and a cigarette are the troika of contentment for him. Admittedly the pint would have to be German or Czech, the book something by Nietzsche and the cigarette from a packet with an animal on the cover. Ed's pleasures are never simple.

I decide to go in. The upstairs section is virtually empty. There are only two men in the pub; both have pint and newspaper in hand. I order a pint and sit down on a comfy sofa, have a sip or two and fish around in my bag for today's copy of the *Guardian*. By the time I've read the headlines, Ed enters, a small rucksack on his back and a book in his coat pocket. The book has been placed so carefully that the title just peeps over the top of the pocket. I have to strain my eyes: *A Critique of Pure Reason* by Immanuel Kant. I wonder sometimes whether Ed reads these books or whether he just uses them as magnets for intelligent women. I also wonder if he's fooling any of them. He throws the rucksack down on the sofa and rubs his hands, exclaims, 'Beer' and walks over to the bar.

'How's your day?' he enquires when he returns laden with beer and several packets of salt and vinegar crisps.

'Not bad. I was slaving away in the language lab for most of the day and then I popped by the newspaper office to see the editor.'

'Got an article in the pipeline?'

'Yeah. Trying to write something on proposed funding changes for students.'

My sentence proves to be a catalyst to conversation. We begin to debate the merits of various methods of student funding. I can feel the stares of the other patrons of the pub. The two have now become several, their glances filled with a mixture of hatred and disdain for students. I feel slightly uncomfortable. Soon however our conversation has taken a natural course and we're back to football and women. The stares have moved elsewhere.

'Ed, we should talk about the summer.'

'Sure,' he replies.

'Are you still on for the Grand Tour of Europe?'

'Sure. Shall we leave a week or two after the end of term? Are we going to plan a route or go with the flow?'

I smile at Ed's turn of phrase. I suggest that we begin in Russia and head back from there. He agrees, but begins to ask me about current developments in Russia. I don my expert's hat and waffle on about the current faction feuds in the Kremlin.

'You don't mind travelling with my sister and her boy-friend, do you?'

My question is hopeful and expectant. Ed had assented months ago, but a mandate taken months ago doesn't always still retain legitimacy.

Ed takes a sip from his pint.

'Course I don't mind. I like your sister.' He takes an-other sip and adds, 'As long as they appreciate, there are places we want to visit, places like Kaliningrad, Krakow, and Klaipeda. We've talked about going to these places for ages. I am not prepared to miss them out, especially Kant's city.'

I smile and nod, not just at Ed's agreement to our trav-elling companions, but at his eloquent alliteration. The intellectuals, or at least the pseudo-intellectuals, will fulfil their wishes, their long-held desires. If the others want to come along for the ride they can.

'Hiyaah!' My sister announces her arrival with her usual greeting to her one and only brother.

'This is Ed.'

'Hi.'

'Hi.'

Standing next to Clara is my sister's boyfriend. Mick is tall. He is wearing a white tight T-shirt that displays his rippling muscles. I can see why Clara finds him very attractive. She introduces him to Ed. Mick sits down after getting a pint of lager and a half for my sister. He begins to tell us about his journey down to London. Ed looks bored. He begins to look in his rucksack, finds his diary and begins to look through it as if he may have forgotten an important appointment. After scanning through seemingly hundreds of pages he puts his diary back into his bag and takes out a large book.

'I bought this today. Thought it would be useful.'

He passes it over to Clara. She smiles. Mick leans across and frowns.

'What is it?'

'A book.'

'Very funny, Ed,' Mick replies sarcastically. He leans over Clara's shoulder and twists the cover towards his face. 'Ah. A guidebook!' He clears his throat and adds, 'I thought you guys knew everything already.'

M UM INTERRUPTS ME in my musings. I was thinking about Radka, my Prague Rose. Mum looks slightly perplexed, a frown stamped upon her face. She asks where Dad is. No doubt he is upstairs playing around with his latest gadget. He doesn't like large gatherings. He is a teacher by day. By night, he likes to get away from people, or at least people he feels obliged to talk to. I find him upstairs. He apologises for leaving us for a few minutes, but, he informs me, the bathroom rail had become disconnected and needed to be repaired. Any old excuse.

There is a queue for the toilet. Martin, my fourteen-year-old cousin, is standing there, his legs crossed, a pained expression on his face and odd squeals emanating from his mouth. I implore Dad to leave his DIY, let everyone relieve himself or herself in peace and go and talk to the assorted collection of relatives. Dad gives me a 'I don't really want to do that' expression and walks off in a sulk. Who is the child now?

Susi is also waiting. Her red dress is more appealing than ever. My beer goggles have put all those not-quite-perfect aspects of the lovely Susi out of focus. I feel rather horny. I am not that drunk. Besides, my parents are downstairs and Ed is no doubt lurking somewhere waiting to try his luck again. Susi engages me in a political discussion. She muses aloud about whether Stalin really was a nasty piece of work. It seems a strange topic. Normally I would leap at the chance to discuss the intricacies of Soviet history, but I know that, after a few beers, political discussions with attractive women are not particularly enlightening. One's mind is thinking about other things. But I have promised Ed to help him this evening, so I have to fob her off with an excuse, something like, 'I would love to discuss this now, but I'm supposed to mingle.' She doesn't seem to mind, she is now at the front of the queue and thinking about other bodily activities.

I return downstairs. Auntie Jean has started to converse with Ed. I'm intrigued to know the topic. I walk past them, my ears strained. I catch the words Assam and jasmine. They are talking about tea. My conspiratorial mind wonders whether they are engaged in some secret plot, the names of varieties of tea being the code words. I've been studying Russian history for too long.

With can of beer in hand, Mick comes into the room. Ed is cut off in mid-flow. He looks over towards Mick and nods, Mick nods in return. No words, no handshakes. These guys spent six weeks travelling together. True, time fades memory, but why don't they at least pass the time of day? Ed, it seems, prefers to talk about tea with my Auntie Jean.

LONDON HEATHROW, TWELVE thirty exactly. Ed is already there. He has a huge rucksack, bulging with socks and books, a copy of *The Guardian* and *Crime and Punishment* in his left hand. As Mick, Clara and I arrive, he smiles and shouts, 'Howdy Traveller!' in a loud American accent. The other passengers in the queue for the flight to Moscow look around. The Russian travellers, looking around, wonder what type of person their country is now letting in. The English look uncomfortable because some-one is speaking too loudly. Ed's humour is an acquired taste. I'm a connoisseur, however, and begin to speak in a range of silly voices. Clara and Mick join the English contingent, except their uncomfortable looks are mingled with a 'we don't really know them' expression.

I begin to teach Ed a few words of Russian. He gets the hang of it very quickly; in no time at all, he can say hello, goodbye, ask for a cup of tea and a beer, and ask where the toilets are.

'Excuse me. Are you flying to Moscow?'

The question emanates from the mouth of a large man sitting opposite. His accent is full of rich Slavic vowels.

'Yes,' I say.

'Just to Moscow?

'No, we'll go on to St Petersburg later.'

'Are you English?'

'Yes.'

'That is good,' he says. 'I love to speak... eh... the English... but I... don't have... chance very often. May I speak to you?'

'Of course' I reply.

Although I want to speak Russian, I console myself with the fact that Ed, Clara and Mick may consider that rude, besides he seems a jolly fellow. We talk for several minutes. It turns out that he works for Gazprom, the Russian utility giant. He has been in London on a brief business trip. Suddenly he stops in mid-sentence, a shocked expression crossing his face. He fishes around in his wallet, he gives me his business card and tells me that he must 'buy... my woman... some... English... eh... presents.' Off he runs. The poor old soul has forgotten to get 'she who must be obeyed' a gift.

My sense of excitement is mounting. In three hours I will be in Moscow. Two years of studying Russian and I will finally be stepping foot on Russian soil. Should I kiss the ground when I arrive? I decide not to. I'm neither the pope nor a long-lost Russian. I wonder whether I will be kissing anything else? It puts a spring in my step. I put my hand on my stomach for the umpteenth time in the last five minutes, not because I've got pains, but just to check that my passport is still in my money-belt. It is. Just relax, Tom! Don't think about crime; think about Red Square, St Basil's and vodka.

Clara has been watching one of the departure monitors for ages. She is transfixed. She doesn't want to miss the flight. She seems to think that if her gaze is momentarily shifted from the screen, we will all miss the flight and our holiday would be in tatters. Mick, meanwhile, is munching away on an apple and consuming his last can of some dodgy lager. An elegant Russian woman with a huge pearl necklace is looking disdainfully at the muscular creature to her right. She plays to the audience, which she knows is watching her, by shifting her handbag from right to left, out of harm's way. She even manages a little cough, or is it a grunt, while performing her manoeuvre. I cannot help but smile.

Clara rouses me from my slumber.

'Come on! Come on!' she implores me. 'The gate has been called!'

Clara seems to think that the stopwatches have started and that we have only one minute to get to the gate before the drawbridge is raised

'Come on, Ed! Stop farting around! Mick! Stop drinking that beer and get a move on! God! Honestly!'

As my sister runs off towards the gate, Ed and I exchange knowing glances.

D AD HAS DECIDED to light the barbecue. Another excuse to avoid the horrors of polite conversation. He is in the garage looking for something. He is standing on the stepladder glancing around to see if whatever it is, is there. I ask Dad if he needs a hand, but he wafts his hand about and tells me not to worry. Not to worry about what I wonder? That my dad seems to invent any excuse not to talk to other humans?

'Aha!' exclaims Dad. The tone suggests a great discovery. The meaning of life? The proof of God's existence? Or maybe the reason why parents are embarrassing? He emerges from the garage with a beaming smile across his face and a rather rusty can of some flammable liquid in his left hand. He strides purposefully through the throng, puts the can down beside the barbecue and rubs his hands in glee. He looks like a witch preparing a special potion as he pours the liquid over the jet-black charcoal. He rubs his hands in glee a second time. Maybe he thinks that friction will ignite the fire. A match is struck. Dad emits a corny, 'Hey presto!' and the fire is lit.

'Sausages.'

'What?' I'm completely taken by surprise by Dad's remark.

'Sausages! Have we got any sausages?'

'Um. Dunno.'

'What about burgers?'

'You mean to say that you have spent half an hour setting up the barbecue and you haven't checked whether you've got any food to cook?'

Dad seems to ignore the sarcastic tone, but he hears the words. He knows that the local store doesn't close until midnight.

'I'm just popping out. Won't be long!'

With that he is gone.

'Where the bloody hell's your dad going?'

'To get sausages for the barbecue, Mum.'

'I'll bloody barbecue him when he gets back!'

MICK FALLS ASLEEP straight away. It has been a long day. Ed is standing by the window watching an altercation between two men. One is short and stocky, the other tall and terribly thin. Both have their hands on a bottle with some colourless potion in it. A black cat struts past them, stares up at them with an air of superiority, emits a meow and proceeds on its way. Ed takes another sip of his beer, puts his hand into his trouser pocket and nods his head. He seems content.

I am too excited to sleep, I feel like a small child who is waiting for his stocking on Christmas Eve. I can't wait. Tomorrow we can start to explore this great city, but why can't tomorrow start today? Ed informs me that he's ready to crash; I just want to keep driving.

*

I first met Ed in the autumn of 1991. I cannot remember much of our first meeting; the huge quantities of beer probably had something to do with it. Ed was standing by the window, much as he is now, a bottle of beer in his hand, gazing at the street below. He was standing by the pool table; his opponent in battle was sizing up his shot.

'Who's on next?' I asked.

The two players fixed their glare on me and then looked at each other. Neither said a word.

'Can I play the winner?'

I thought maybe an extra sentence might stimulate some kind of a response from the two hustlers. Both nodded the same length and type of nod as if they were a pair of synchronised swimmers. Not an auspicious start, I thought, but the first week of term is always a time to throw oneself headlong into the deep end, even if on occasions one ends up diving into an empty pool and cracking open one's skull.

'So,' I began rather timidly. Thoughts raced around in my mind. Topics of conversation swirled around. Study? No, too boring. Women? That would have made me sound desperate. Politics? Never a good way to kick off a conversation. Let others raise the issues, then argue. I opted instead for an easy topic: pool. For the first few minutes I just talked about how bad I was at pool. Looks of suspicion graced their faces. Is he for real or is he just a hustler?

Their looks of scepticism only dissipated after I had lost my first game. Nobody, not even the best hustlers, would hit the cue ball off the table twice and accidentally pot the black with his third shot. I burst out laughing and they found my laugh infectious. I then promised to make amends for my appalling display of pool playing and do something I had some aptitude for like buying a round of drinks.

DAD ARRIVES BACK with a beaming grin on his face. He is laden with goodies. He puts his bags down next to the barbecue and begins to rummage around in one of them. As quick as a flash, a 'dad' expression if ever there was one, he pulls something out of the bag. There is a loud bang and strands of paper are falling on my head. Before I have to time to register the fact that Dad is letting off party poppers, Auntie Jean has been covered in strands of paper too. Much laughter ensues. For a man who seems to hate gatherings of people, Dad knows how to liven up a party.

After setting off a few more, he passes the box to Cousin Martin and orders him to go forth and wreak havoc. Dad rubs his hands in glee and begins to open up the packs of sausages and burgers. He has even thoughtfully bought a packet of veggie burgers for Clara. She's decided to stop eating red meat, after watching a documentary on the TV. Dad's mad, but considerate.

People have started to gather round like vultures; they know food is on the agenda and know their desires will soon be fulfilled.

My legs wander off to the shed at the bottom of the garden. My mind wanders back to that evening of sheer delight with Radka, sexy Radka.

'LET'S TRY THIS one,' says Ed, his voice full of enthusiasm.

'Um.' I am rather non-committal in my response.

Clara, on the other, seems intrigued by the façade and the clientele. I am surprised that she wants to try this dingy café. A man, cigarette in mouth and empty vodka bottle in his left hand, stumbles out of the door.

Our prevarications end when Mick informs us that he is 'fucking hungry' and asks, 'Why the fuck don't we just go in and fucking eat?' Mick's turn of phrase may be at times a little vulgar, but like any good worker he forces the chattering classes to get off their backsides and do something. On closer inspection it is a self-service restaurant for the down-and-outs of St Petersburg. I inform everyone that after three days of doing all the talking, I want the others to get the food, while I nab the table which has just been vacated by a woman of spectacular girth. Mick tells me he'll join me. The other two agree to get food for the four of us.

Ed and Clara queue patiently, while an old Russian man, a dog in tow, talks to the assistant about his daughter, I feel privileged to understand the witterings of this old man. Clara and Ed, in contrast, cannot understand anything. They probably think that this old man can't make up his mind what to eat. Ed looks at Clara. His expression is one of bafflement. He wonders what to do. Should he barge through? Ask the old man to continue his conversation at a more convenient time? Or just wait? Ed is desperate to know what is the done thing. Eventually, the old man turns round, sees my two travelling companions, and issues an apology. His beautiful rich accent carries the meaning; there is no need to translate. He beckons them forward, imploring them to order.

Ed begins by wishing the woman behind the counter good day. He does it out of politeness, but it is a crowd pleaser. His accent is good, but his stumbling delivery cannot hide his origins. He is clearly a foreigner.

'Please,' he says in Russian. 'I would like,' he continues in Russian. He repeats the line again, but adds in English, 'One of those sausages.'

The assistant is baffled. She asks him what he wants. I understand, but Ed is perplexed; she could be asking for proof of the theory of relativity for all he knows. Ed points at the sausages. The assistant points at the bread. The old man joins in; he has a friendly avuncular manner. He wants to help Ed and Clara. The old man starts to point at the soup. Ed shakes his head and points in the direction of the sausages. The assistant is smiling. She signals for Ed to come round the counter. The old man follows him. The dog just sits there motionless, unaware that he understands as much as everyone else. Mick implores me to go over and give them a hand. He reminds me he is hungry. Ed, however, is having a ball; I don't want to stop him.

Clara has started to join in. She is pointing at the soup and asking, 'How much?'

The shop assistant is dumbfounded. Clara takes out a small denomination note and points at the soup. Revelation! She looks around for a piece of paper and writes down a figure. Clara nods and holds up four fingers. The assistant points at the rolls. Clara nods and holds up another four fingers. The scene resembles a farce from the days of silent movies. Ed is laughing and so is the avuncular old man.

Ed and Clara bound up to our table, with trays laden with goods. They have huge grins emblazoned across their faces. I can see the funny side, Mick cannot.

I GLANCE AT my watch. People are already beginning to leave. I have spent the last twenty minutes saying goodbye to half of my guests. They leave, mumbling lines about the volume of traffic, how Angela is going on holiday tomorrow and that they have an early start tomorrow. Judy and David come up, shake my hand and say something about what an enjoyable evening they have had, but that they must be on their way. Their body language, however, suggests a different story. David, an old friend from schooldays, wants to stay on. His handshake lasts much longer, he talks more of his enjoyable evening than the pressing timetable. Judy, his fiancée, has a false smile imprinted on her face. She doesn't want to offend me, but she feels they ought to be hitting the road. David starts to talk with great enthusiasm about the plans for their wedding. Judy's smile starts to wane. She slips her hand surreptitiously into David's and exerts a slight, but discernible tug. David stops in mid-sentence and tells me that he must be off. She keeps hold of him all the way to the front door.

Dad has donned his blue-striped apron. The aroma of sizzling sausages has drawn a large crowd. Mick and Clara are standing hand in hand next to the barbecue, their stares fixed on the flickering flames. Clara looks fatigued; she is resting her head on the shoulders of her boyfriend, not primarily out of affection, but because she wishes to rest her weary head.

Those guests who are staying have moved on from beer and wine to either spirits or coffee, depending on whether they want to return to the safe shores of sobriety or strike out to the undisclosed waters of drunkenness. I have poured myself a vodka and coke. Just a splash of vodka emits such a reek that I can pass off my drink as potent even though it contains a mere drop or two of the magic potion. I know that I have to walk a tightrope. I cannot look as if I'm not drinking on this day, this very special day, but equally, as so many of my relatives are still here, I can't do anything foolish in their eyes. Oh the quandaries of being a host!

'Hello,' says an all too familiar voice. Ed is standing next to me holding a bottle of beer in one hand and a half-empty bottle of wine in the other.

'How ya doin'?'

'Awight. Been trying me luck with the', his voice suddenly takes on a distinguished tone, 'delectable Susi.'

'Any luck?'

'Well, I have seen off that young upstart, Fred,' he adds in a Oxford accent. 'I told him to go and satisfy his lust elsewhere.'

'You didn't need to be that harsh!' I reply without a silly accent.

'He's such a twat, though,' replies Ed in his normal voice. 'I mean anyone who waffles on and on about Kant's categorical imperative and doesn't even recognise his debt to Rousseau should be shot.'

'That's how I usually feel,' I retort sarcastically. Most people would wish to shoot Ed for his pretentious philosophical indulgence.

'I'm starving! When will the burgers be ready?'

'Soon.'

Dad takes out a bag of rolls from his bag and picks up a kitchen knife. He is ready to serve up his culinary delights.

'Mick! Mick!' he shouts, while simultaneously beckoning my sister's headrest towards him. 'Come and cut these rolls for me. I only have *one* pair of hands, you know!'

Mick wanders over and picks up the knife. He raises it to eye level and flicks it over in his hand. I turn round; Ed is making his way to the house.

'Where are you going? The food is ready.'

'I'm desperate for the Gents'.'

I T IS SEVEN thirty in the evening. Ed is sitting opposite munching away on some sausages. Mick is reading the guidebook, while Clara rests her head on his left shoulder. We are waiting, waiting for our train, the train that will take us out of St Petersburg and on to Tallinn, the capital of Estonia. It will be a shame to leave this beautiful city and this fascinating country. We have spent a mere week in this land, a mere seven days, and yet I feel as if I have been here for years. Our train leaves at nine. I decide to wander around and try to savour the final ninety minutes of St Petersburg.

A young boy is racing around, shouting at his mother, demanding that she plays with him. The mother is sitting on a bench, piles of clothes all around her. I offer her a greeting, she responds in kind. I smile and move on. Eighty-nine minutes and counting.

The queue at the ticket booths is long and winding. The station has fifty booths, but only three are open. A *babushka* is shouting at a man in front of her in the queue demanding to know why he pushed in. The man, sporting a five o'clock shadow as shady as Nixon, offers some tame excuse. He is guilty, but he will not budge.

Outside, on platform one, I see a beautiful woman. She has rich dark eyes and a small nose. Should I speak to her? It would after all only be an ephemeral experience. But what the hell, life is ephemeral. At times you've got to seize the moment, seize the day.

'Excuse me,' I say cautiously, 'do you know where I can buy a newspaper?'

It is a banal question, but at least I don't ask where the toilets are, or when the next train leaves for Moscow. She has a newspaper under her arm, I am half hoping she will donate it to me.

'I am sorry, but I don't know,' she replies politely.

I linger for a second, wondering what to ask, when a large Russian man with wall-to-wall muscles strides up the platform and kisses her on the cheek. I begin to slump backwards. The prize has been won by another.

'This man wants to buy a newspaper,' she informs her lover while pointing at me. The man smiles, displays his set of sparkling teeth reminiscent of a toothpaste advert, and hands me his copy of *Izvestiya*. I thank them and continue on my wander. At least I have a consolation prize. Eighty minutes and counting.

At the end of the platform an old man is sitting down on a bench and clutching a bottle of some colourless liquid. He beckons me over. His breath reeks of alcohol. His shabby coat is torn along the back and is bereft of two buttons. I sit beside him. He passes me his bottle and implores me to drink. I decline. He seems taken aback. I rise from the bench, walk over to the nearest kiosk and buy a bottle of beer. As I return with my bottle of fun-inducing, funny-tasting liquid, I sit down next to him, carefully avoiding doing any damage to his coat.

'Where ya heading?' he asks, his words merging together. He leans across and stares at me. All I can see are dilated pupils.

'Tallinn,' I reply.

The man emits a grunt, nods, rocks back and forward. He throws some more liquid down his gullet and wipes his mouth with the sleeve of his stained jacket. I smile nervously. He stretches out his right hand and places it on my shoulder. He opens his mouth, displays his need for an orthodontist and asks, 'Why?'

Before I have a chance to reply, he closes his eyes, smiles and slumps back. I hear snoring. Was I that boring to talk to? Is my voice really so soporific? Seventy minutes and counting.

Outside the station the good citizens of St Petersburg are going about their business. Battered buses that have seen thousands of passengers getting on and off trundle up and down the street and emit a dirty black smoke. Two stray dogs run across the road, frightened looks on their unwashed faces. A BMW drives past at speed, followed by a police motorcycle. The pedestrians stop in their tracks and gaze at this phenomenon. Discussion ensues, but after a couple of questions and unsatisfactory speculative answers, the topic of conversation returns to normal, more important things. Fifty minutes and still counting.

Mick is thoughtfully cutting up the sausages into handy bite-sized chunks with his knife. Clara leans back, rests her weary head against his pectoral muscles, brings her eyelids together, and savours the taste of a Russian sausage. Mick leans back, a look of sheer contentment gracing his face. Twenty-five minutes. The seconds are ticking away.

A neon sign beckons me over. I am drawn by the hint of the unusual, the exotic. Two other characters have been entrapped. One can charitably be described as plump; his T-shirt tries its best, but cannot cover up his stomach. He is sipping a beer and staring into oblivion. I cross his line of vision, but nothing registers, the radar is blank. The other man sees me approaching, grabs his bottle of beer and pulls it to towards him. He has his eyes on the prize. No man will deprive him of his liquid refreshment. I greet the assistant in the kiosk. He returns the greeting curtly and without any genuine feeling. He doesn't wish one health, just a healthy appetite. I order an open sandwich and a beer. Swiftly, a beer is put in front of me. 'Cheers!' The man to my left lifts his bottle in response to my salutation. He cannot manage the words, but his sentiment is warm. He looks precariously balanced on his seat and not too sure of his movements. I don't want him to fall off and injure himself just to salute a foreigner. I smile as broadly as I can, raise my bottle and return to my fellow travellers.

I feel we are closing a chapter. Our journey is not even a quarter gone and yet, as I wander around the station, the sense of movement to a new place grasps me. Suitcases, bags, cages for animals, bundles of clothes tied with fraying rope, all seem to signify the exit of the players from the stage. Tomorrow there will be new actors playing their parts, entering through the doors to my left, while we shall leave through the doors to the right. Some come to welcome newcomers, others to say goodbye. I know I will return.

SUSI BIDS ME farewell. She must be off. She is going to Edinburgh tomorrow. She smiles and asks me to escort her to the door. I oblige. How can I refuse such an offer? Before she gets to the front door, she asks to have a look at my room. I cannot decline. I lead her upstairs into my room, my pad. A feeling of horror engulfs me. Everything objectively cool I own is in my new place in London. All my uncool tapes, however, are here and clearly visible. The Pet Shop Boys stare back at me. I am sure that Susi's eyes will focus on this piece of incriminating evidence. I am guilty of objective bad taste.

When I turn round, however, she shows no interest in my tape collection. She shuts the door with the heel of her shoe, grabs my trousers and starts to kiss my face. I am rapidly aroused. She grabs my head and thrusts hers towards mine. This is not a good time! This is not a good time! This is not a good time! My God! My parents are downstairs! Ed, my best friend, is somewhere in the vicinity, searching for the object of his desire. How can I do this? Oh, my God! Oh, my God! Fuck! No, that's exactly what I don't want to do! Bollocks! Oh please, please! Her hand has moved round from the back to the front of my trousers. She is moving it up and down. My breathing involuntarily deepens. I am slipping down the slope. I need to be rescued. Susi slumps to her knees and begins to undo my belt. What should I do?

'Tom! Tom! Your Auntie Jean wants to say goodbye! Where are you?'

Thank God for Mum. She has saved me from an awful situation. I really wanted to continue, but it would have been fleeting pleasure, with long-term pain. As Dad says, 'You win some and you lose some.' Thank God for parents.

Ed is standing by the window overlooking the back garden. Night has fallen. Only the light from the barbecue's flames and Dad's super-special, all-purpose lamp is visible. Ed looks melancholy. His eyes are fixed on the scene below, but he doesn't want to join in.

'Why don't you grab something to eat?'

'I don't feel hungry any more.'

'But you said a few minutes ago that you were starving.'

'Well, I... I... I've lost my appetite.'

'What's the matter?'

'Nothing.'

'Is it Susi?'

'God, no!'

'Well what?'

'Nothing,' he intones. He clearly doesn't want to talk about it.

'Look, what is it? Is it Mick?'

'What makes you say that?'

'You've acted really strange today whenever he's been around. What is it?'

'I can't explain it to you, maybe one day I will, but not today.' With that he pats me on the shoulder, thanks me for a great party and walks out the door.

Part Two
Train Hopping

CLARA LOVES TRAINS, she thinks they are romantic. She has good cause. She can be very chatty at times, especially if she has nothing better to do. Long train journeys provide her with ample opportunities to natter.

Four years ago she was travelling from London to Cheltenham. It was Christmas Eve. The carriages were full to the brim with suitcases, rucksacks, boxes of presents and a deluge of people. In amongst the assorted mass sat my sister. She had prudently reserved a seat. The eyes of envy watched her from all sides. She wondered whether she should give up her seat for the young mother standing by the train door. Children were rushing around, screaming. She decided against such a move. She had spent her lunch hour the previous Thursday queuing and booking her ticket. She deserved her comfort.

After polishing off the *Daily Mail*, she gazed around for something to do. The train had only been in motion for twenty-five minutes, another ninety awaited her. The green and pleasant land was rushing past the window at one hundred miles an hour. Idyllic villages were past in a second. Herds of cattle lay motionless on the ground. Flakes of snow whirled around, disorientated by the velocity of the people transporter. Christmas beckoned. Visions of turkey, port, TV, and Granny's Christmas pudding wafted through her mind like break-dancing dung-beetles.

Reading was the first port of call, or as the dear announcer called it, 'our next station stop'. The train eased into the station five minutes late. Huge numbers of people left the train at Reading, including the young mum who had troubled Clara's conscience. She smiled a smile of relief, wriggled her shoulders and closed her eyes. Time to think about Christmas again.

'Excuse me! I've reserved this seat!'

The woman opposite was having an argument with a tall man. They were showing each other their tickets. The woman started to raise her voice.

'I've reserved this seat! I'm not as young as I used to be you know! I fought in the war you know!'

'But I booked it! Look at my ticket!'

The young man shoved the ticket into the old woman's face. She was not going to budge. He looked towards Clara. Maybe there might exist some solidarity of youth.

'Look!' he said, thrusting his seat reservation towards Clara. She perused it for a second. Date, time, seat number; everything seemed to be in order.

'This seems right. Can I have a look at yours?' asked Clara.

The old lady reluctantly handed over her ticket.

'Ah! Look! The time is wrong. You must've reserved a seat on an earlier train.'

The old lady snatched the ticket back, stared at it for a couple of seconds, gathered up her things and projected her icy cold stare at my sister. All her annoyance, all her hatred, was encapsulated in that stare. She rose trying to maintain her dignity. She muttered something about the youth of today having no respect for their elders and left.

'Outrageous! She was totally out of order!' exclaimed the young male. He took off his rucksack, flung it on to the luggage rack and plonked himself down on the seat, his well-earned reward. 'Thanks a lot,' he said, a broad smile accompanying his expression of gratitude. 'By the way, my name's Mick.'

Clara's first boyfriend was Matt. He was the kind of boyfriend parents like. He came from good stock. His father was a doctor, his mother a teacher. He could talk to my dad about wine, to my mum about opera. He also ate whatever my mum offered him. He was full of ambition, wanting to follow in his dad's footsteps. Mum was planning the wedding from the day Matt first came for supper.

Matt, however, was *too* good. He always drove my sister home by eleven thirty. He never allowed her to drink too much. He never invited her for a dirty weekend. He probably never even dreamed of sleeping with her, but there are certain things a sister doesn't tell you and there are certain things you don't want to know.

I didn't like Matt because he agreed with everything my dad said. Admittedly when it is your first dinner at the girlfriend's parents' house, you tend to nod your head in agreement to every single view they espouse. Hanging? Yes! Beggars should be locked up? Of course! Adolf Hitler? Fine chap, much misunderstood. After a while, however, you should feel more at ease and confident enough to deviate from blind obedience. Not necessarily to disagree violently with every word uttered, but just the occasional word of discord. Hanging only for serial murders, more heavy-handed measures against beggars and saying that Hitler would have been better off with less facial hair.

But Matt never uttered a word of disagreement. Mum, Dad and I gradually came to despise this automaton. We started to play cruel games. I remember one evening in particular. Matt arrived at around six. He spent half an hour upstairs in Clara's room, but obediently brought her down when supper was called. Dad exchanged pleasantries and pleasant chit-chat while we ate a bowl of piping hot tomato soup. It was when the spag bol – or spaghetti bolognese as Mum had insisted on calling it ever since she started Italian lessons at night school – arrived that Dad began to launch into political discussion. He turned to Matt and asked, 'What do you think about the Star Wars project then?'

'Star Wars?' replied Matt. His tone was questioning. He couldn't understand why my dad was asking him about Luke Skywalker and Darth Vader. He looked towards my sister for help, but Clara was engrossed in her food; she couldn't get one particular strand of spaghetti to stay on her fork. In desperation Matt looked at me. I could feel those eyes pleading with me.

'You know, the Strategic Defense Initiative, so that the Americans will be able to shoot down Soviet missiles before they land on the land of the free.'

'Um. I...'

Matt looked around again, but I sat there motionless and Clara was still troubled by that strand of spaghetti.

'I think it is a very good idea. Anything to keep the Soviet Union away from the West.'

'Do you really think that the Soviet Union is so pernicious?' asked Dad.

'Um.' Matt was squirming. 'Um,' he repeated. 'Well... Um...'

'I think that the Soviet Union is the most benign country in the world,' added Dad.

His voice betrayed no hint of irony, but he and I knew he was playing games. Matt couldn't bring himself to express anything verbally, but he nodded his head.

'I think after supper we should make effigies of Ronald Reagan and George Bush and burn them. And while we watch them burn we ought to link hands and sing *The Red Flag*.' He paused for dramatic effect. 'Don't you agree, Tom?'

I voiced my approval and watched Matt's face. His gulp was audible. 'What about you, Matt?'

'Yes, Mr Reed. You must excuse me, but I must...'

He got up mumbled his last few words and went to the toilet. He stayed there nearly ten minutes.

Dinner at our place became a far more infrequent affair after that evening. They split soon afterwards. I am not proud of the way I acted, but he was asking for it. You can't put a bait like that in front of Dad and me and expect it to stay there while we salivate.

I AM WOKEN by a noise. My watch, thanks to its luminous display, beams back 05.45 at me. I raise my head. Ed is lying on the floor, his rucksack under his head like a king-sized pillow. Mick is lying on the seat opposite. He has wrapped all his spare jumpers around himself. He looks rather silly, but then I'm sure I wouldn't win a fashion contest at the moment.

Clara isn't in the compartment. My God! Clara isn't in the compartment! Where is she? I jump up and open the compartment door. Where can she be? I hope she's all right. I look to the left. Nothing. I look the other way, still no sign. I pull up the laces on my boots and begin to tie them. Where can she? Oh my, I hope, maybe...

'Hello.'

Clara is standing there.

'Where've you been?'

'Just went for a quick wander.'

'I was worried.'

'Needn't have been. Come and have a look at the beginnings of the sunrise.'

We stand and chat for nearly half an hour, giggling about the time Dad tried to cook a Sunday roast and set off all the smoke alarms. The neighbours were so worried about us that they called the fire brigade. Still, Dad did at least manage to serve the firemen a portion of sherry trifle.

'How are you finding the trip?' I ask.

'It's been great. I loved St Petersburg, especially the episode in the café. That was brilliant.'

'How are things with Mick?'

'Really great. You know, I think I might marry him.'

'Really?'

'Yeah.'

It seems a fitting end to the conversation. The sun has crept over the horizon, farmers are already in the fields, tractors have been started, cattle have risen from their slumber. Another day has begun. Another day just like the last and the thousands before that.

I AM ROUSED from my slumber by a loud thud on the door. Before I have time to think about an answer, Clara is standing over me, a mug of tea in her left hand.

'Morning! Up you get! You've got loads of clearing up to do!'

How can my sister be so sprightly at this hour? I glance at my watch. It is already afternoon. I promised Mum that I would clear up the mess wrought by the party-goers by seven thirty. She has got one of her opera appreciation society meetings tonight. Wing Commander Forbes wouldn't want to have cans of beer strewn all over the floor, while he explains the lyrical significance of *Turandot*.

I reach out and grasp the mug full to the brim of tea. I try to drink the tea while lying horizontally. My brain is telling my hand and mouth that such an operation cannot be completed without a hitch or two. I manage to spill some of the tea over my duvet. I feel stupid. Why don't I listen to my brain sometimes? I am a rational, cerebral type of fellow, so why does my body decide to rebel against the laws proscribed by my brain? Is it just trying to be bloody-minded? Or is just my brain's ploy to make me realise what a clever organ it is? Perhaps the body has double agents in my mind? Double bluffs, deception and spies. It is all too much for the first moments of my day.

My sister has never brought me a cup of tea in bed before. I don't normally have such thoughts about my brain in the morning. I don't usually have impossible tasks like clearing up by seven thirty. Today is going to be a trial of strength. I feel like a dog.

The scene downstairs is desperate. Mum and Clara quite rightly refuse to clear up any of the mess. I wanted to have a party. I have to pay the price and the price is a day of cleaning.

I wander into the kitchen only to see beer cans. Last night was obviously Attack of the Beer Cans. They are everywhere: on top of the fridge, on the window sill, in the sink, on the floor. The sight of all this beer is nauseating. I find a black plastic bin liner and begin to throw the cans in one after another, but after a couple of minutes, I slump on to the chair. I cannot go on. I try to wish the rubbish away.

'Chop-chop!'

It's Dad in one of his jolly moods.

KLAIPEDA ISN'T MOST people's idea of an ideal seaside resort, but then I have odd tastes. This small town stuck on the Baltic coast was once the German town, Memel. The only point of interest is a small decaying theatre which displays its best side to the female statue in the centre of the stage. The statue looks unimpressed. So what if Hitler announced *Anschluss* of the German Reich with Memel from the balcony?

What have you done for me recently?

Mick and Clara aren't impressed. Ed is wandering around gazing up at the buildings, but I imagine that he is just trying to give me the impression of captivation. His stomach is probably rumbling, his body in desperate need of a cup of tea. Still he wanders around gazing and gasping. His acting is terrible, but his sentiments are decent.

Today is one of those awkward days. I wanted to come to Klaipeda, but the others didn't. Clara is egging us on toward the south and the sun, whereas Ed is desperate to visit the home of his intellectual hero, Immanuel Kant. I am depriving them of their happiness, but what else can I do? Ever since I first heard about this small town, I have wanted to visit it. I am not depriving them of their liberty; they can go on alone if they so wish, but if they want me to accompany them, they must wait. I am their translator, their guide, their eyes and their ears. They have entered into a contract with me; they have received the benefits, now they must pay the price.

Mick wanders up to me and inquires, with more than a hint of desperation in his voice, 'So, what's so special about this place again?' His question suggests that maybe this time, the fourth, I think, he might be enlightened. I begin to explain the build-up to the Second World War, the rise of Nazism and the plans to unite all the German speakers into a single country, creating a new Reich.

Mick feigns interest. He nods, grunts and looks around at the buildings. His mind is probably desperately trying to fathom out why this person, his girlfriend's brother, is so captivated by a desperately ordinary square in a small, seemingly insignificant town on the Baltic coast. Mick nods again and wanders off, still staring at the buildings. Mick and Ed both fail to appreciate that significance often lies in places that seem at first totally insignificant.

After nearly half an hour in the square, my travelling companions have their prayer answered. Spots of rain begin to fall from the heavens. As if to emphasise the point, Ed, Clara and Mick decide to have a race to see who can put their waterproof on first. Mick wins hands down; he has sensibly put his coat at the top of his rucksack.

Clara suggests that we go and grab a coffee, a suggestion to which we all consent. We wander through the back streets, the quiet back streets of Klaipeda. Clara spots a suitable café and in we march behind our new sergeant major. Clara suggests that I find a table while she goes to see what there is on offer. Mick plonks himself down beside me, but his gaze is fixed on my sibling. Clara nods at a waiter. She is smiling, pointing and saying in very slow and deliberate English, 'What is that?' Her 'a' seems interminable. Ed is smiling, nodding and pointing. He remembers the eating joint in St Petersburg. He wants to repeat the experience. Clara's head is nodding incessantly; every two seconds she seems to emit another 'yeah!'

A friendly-looking soul in a smart suit comes up and says, 'Yes. I can help you. What… um, do you want?'

Clara looks around, her set of sparkling white teeth on display for all.

'How about some of this? And this?'

Ed and Clara nod. Their trays are filled with goodies in no time. As they approach the cash desk, Clara looks round at Ed, smiles and pats him on the shoulder. They approach our table. Their happiness is palpable. Who dares wins.

T ODAY IS THE morning after the morning after. The birthday party is already slipping into the further recesses of my mind. Fragments of memory remain like used coffee grounds in a filter. The great keeper of memory has run away with the coffee. Witty one-liners, those jokes that one makes and wishes to use again, have been whisked away, never to return. All I can remember are the embarrassing moments. Not all the embarrassing moments are mine, I hasten to add.

Susi has invited me to Edinburgh for the weekend. She is performing for a small theatre company, who are putting on a production of *Waiting for Godot*. The twist that the bright young things have come up with is that the cast is entirely female. Ed finds this appealing for two reasons. Firstly, there is a hint of originality in such a production, but, more importantly, there are no men for Susi to cavort with at the cast parties. He still lives in hope.

I have nothing to do this morning. I have to meet Ed at one o'clock at King's Cross station, but apart from that I feel like Estragon and Vladimir.

The tube is busy. The massed ranks of commuters may be already ensconced safely in their office buildings, but the carriages are still overflowing as the clock strikes ten. To my left are two Italians sitting and clutching their bags. Their white knuckles are clearly visible to any would-be thief. Opposite sits a pretty tourist with a dark complexion. She is studying the map with great intensity. How any visitor to Britain's capital can fathom the tube map is beyond me. Her glance which was transfixed by the map is diverted only briefly by a quick glance at the map above my head, as if this map (which is identical to hers) will solve her riddle.

I wonder whether I should help this poor lost soul. Let's weigh up the pros and cons. I will lose my seat to the large man standing to my right. He has been watching all our seats like a hawk. Any movement, however slight, and he will go in for the kill. She may not speak English. She may just think I'm trying to chat her up. On the other hand, it would be my good turn for the day. Before I make my decision, she puts her map away, stands up and alights from the carriage. Another moment lost. How many times have I let the moment pass? How I envy those people who just do things. I wish at times I could just strike while the iron is hot, not when it is decidedly lukewarm.

An American couple get on the tube at South Kensington. Their voices carry. The English on the tube look around desperately and then throw their heads into newspapers and hope the volume will be turned down. The Americans, unlike the pretty girl with a dark complexion, muse aloud.

'Which station, honey?'

'It's… Hang on a minute. I have it written down.'

The lady opens her handbag and takes out her purse. It is bulging. She finally finds a scrap of paper with the address on it. She reads it out loud, not just aloud, but loud so that everyone can hear. I wish I could jump up and tell them that a hundred pair of ears can hear. Not all will belong to whiter than white souls. Perhaps I should just remember Tracey's dictum, 'Sometimes you gotta have a little faith in people.' My obsession with spies has pervaded my general outlook.

I travel north, change tubes and end up in Camden. Camden Town is one of those places where one comes to be seen. My attire is very normal. I am not sporting a large colourful hat, or a pair of flares replete with a flowery pattern. In fact, I'm just wearing a blue shirt and a pair of khaki-coloured trousers. I wouldn't turn any heads on the catwalks of Milan, but then I wouldn't want to anyway.

A man stops me by the exit to the tube. He puts out his hand and pats me on the shoulder.

'My friend,' he says, while saliva drips on to my shirt. 'My friend, you couldn't spare me some change?'

I look at the poor, dejected old man. His jacket is in a sorry state. The solitary button remaining is hanging by the last piece of thread. I'm shocked by the symbolism, but instead of giving the old man a charitable few pence, I mutter some rubbish about having nothing and walk away briskly and intently. What a terrible thing to do. Don't I have any heart? I'm struck by a feeling of remorse. Perhaps I should go back. On second thoughts maybe not. I should not look to the past, but try to remember how to act in the future. Oh the perils of a liberal conscience.

It reminds me of a moment in Tallinn, capital of Estonia, during that journey with Ed, Clara and Mick. We had just arrived in the city. We were tired and hungry. If we'd have informed the good citizens of Estonia of our imminent arrival maybe they would have rushed around and brought us some bread and salt as soon as we stepped on to the platform. There was no welcoming party, just the sun beaming down on us, warming the cockles of our dishevelled hearts. We scouted around the station looking for a supermarket.

'Look! Over there! Look!' said Ed, his finger pointing towards a shop of some description. 'That looks promising!'

Ed was ever the optimist. He could see a mass of people queuing. They must be queuing for something. We joined the queue, Ed and I. We eventually made it into the shop, but then our rational thought processes seemed to let us down. There were five separate queues, six shop assistants and a huge pile of bread. Ed looked at me. His face asked me a million questions. I gazed around the shop, surely there must be a system. We studied the shoppers for a minute or so, but we were none the wiser.

'I'll try this one,' I said tentatively.

'Okay. Um… I'll try this one, shall I?'

Ed was pointing at a queue, but he was being elbowed out.

We tried to join another one of the queues, but we were getting nowhere.

'Look! You need one of those tickets!'

'What tickets?' I enquired.

'Those!' exclaimed Ed, his finger stretching out and pointing.

We joined the queue for the tickets and reached the front. I stood there for a second, waiting for the blond-haired assistant to give me a ticket. She looked at me and asked something in Estonian. I was caught in a bind. Should I speak English or Russian? I tried my mother tongue. The woman smiled and shook her head. I'd asked her what I had to do to get bread. It wasn't a yes/no question. I tried Russian. She smiled again. I had deliberately put on an English accent. She knew I wasn't Russian.

I asked again, 'Please can you tell me how I buy some bread. We are very hungry.'

The woman behind us, a classic *babushka* if ever I saw one, started to explain that one needed to queue up in another queue, pick up a ticket, then go over to a second counter and order some bread, then queue up at a third, where one got a ticket with the price written on it, and finally one could go to the cash desk.

Ed and I wondered whether we should give up, but by now we had half the shop on our side. The lovely old *babushka* shouted over to what she called, but which was not labelled, counter number one. A ticket was passed over the heads of the massed ranks of Estonians, over to the counter number two. 'How many? How many?' they shouted. I held up four fingers. The assistant at counter number two passed four loaves over to another assistant. Our assistant, number three, scribbled something on a scrap of paper.

The crowd was engrossed in our purchase. I felt guilty. Here was I, an affluent Englishman, holding up a group of hungry Estonians. The *babushka* raised her stick, the Red Sea of people divided and we proceeded to counter number four and then on to five. As we finally got our hand on the bread, we felt ecstatic. A cheer went up from a few of those waiting. Ed shouted, 'Thank you! Thank you!' at the top of his voice. It would never happen in London.

We stepped out into the hot summer afternoon, our prizes clutched closely to our chests. Clara and Mick were sitting waiting for us on a bench. We strolled over and began to distribute the food.

As we began to munch away, a beggar stumbled up to our bench, his dirty mangy hand outstretched in our direction. He mumbled something. He mumbled again and began pointing to his mouth. We all sat there motionless. He understood the signals and left.

How could I *do* that? He was desperate for food. He was starving. Those kind Estonians in the bread shop had helped me and I couldn't even spare a small hunk of food for a starving man. So much for my liberal conscience. While Ed and I mused over the decline of altruism in modern society and the harrowing message of *The Fall*,

Clara ran after the beggar and donated a small hunk of her bread. She returned triumphant; our heads were bowed in shame.

I T IS ALMOST eleven thirty by the time I arrive at King's Cross station. There was a security alert on the Northern Line. I sat for almost half an hour on the platform at Camden Town station. I wandered along the platform and sat myself down next to a man wearing a dog collar. Not a clerical dog collar, I hasten to add, but an actual dog collar. He was sporting a large red jacket and his face contained so many earrings, nose-rings and eyebrow-rings that I wished I had a magnet. We would have seen who was cool then!

While I sat next to the trendy, a man with a black suit and a mobile phone was running up and down the platform.

'Hi, Ross! It's just fuckin' terrible! God! Fuck! Fucking London Transport! Fuck them!'

Everyone looked at him. Foreign students turned their heads to listen to his vocabulary. They were probably taking notes. The black-suited man ran up to an underground worker and began to shout and bawl at him.

'Call this a fuckin' service? It's a fuckin' disgrace!' The London Underground man nodded, smiled, straightened his orange luminous jacket and picked up his broom.

'I just do the cleaning. It will be here soon. It's a security alert. I think you should blame the IRA, not me.'

Reason and common sense were just not good enough for the complainer. He walked off in a huff and emitted an expletive for every stride he made down the platform.

I feel a tap on my shoulder. Ed is standing there with a huge Texan hat on his head, I gesture towards it. Before words have emanated from my orifice, Ed begins to speak, 'I know, I know what you're thinking, but, well, why not!'

'Yes,' I reply sarcastically in a Paxmanesque tone. We laugh and board the train.

THE TRAIN IS full. An old lady with a walking stick and hand-knitted cardigan hobbles on to the train. She stares up at Ed and me and grins.

'Do you think you could?'

Before she has a chance to finish her question, we follow her train of thought and pick up her battered suitcase.

'Is this free, love?' she enquires of a short man with a short back and sides who is holding a mobile phone.

He nods and reluctantly removes his briefcase from the chair by the aisle. He doesn't want company. He doesn't want to be called 'love' by a total stranger. He wants to remain an atomistic individual.

'Good party, I thought,' says Ed desperate to kick off the conversation.

'Yeah. Thought so.'

'Shame. I couldn't get it on with Susi, you know.'

'Yeah.'

My mind races to images of Susi pressing herself up against my weak and feeble body. I think I'm starting to blush. Suppress it! Suppress it! Stupid sentiments, they only intensify the red spreading across my cheeks.

'Why you blushing?' asks Ed.

My face goes even redder. Why did God, or natural selection, or whatever brought humans on to this earth, make us blush? It seems so terribly cruel.

'I...' I'm at a loss for words. 'I just can't stop myself thinking about Dad rushing around and cooking burgers until three in the morning! Parents are so embarrassing!'

I wonder whether he has fallen for it. I'm not so sure. Ed is a good judge of character. He knows when I'm not telling the truth. He knows when everyone his lying.

'What are you reading at the moment?'

I try to set the conversation off on a new, less hazardous course.

'Kant.'

Heads turn and stare at Ed. An old man shakes his head and mutters. The old lady, whom we had helped with her baggage, emits a 'Really! With children around!' Evidently she thought Ed had been describing the female pudendum.

'You're reading Kant again. I thought you'd read everything by him a million times. Why don't you try something different?'

'Some people have the Bible, I have the *Critique of Pure Reason*.'

Our conversation meanders. We hurl it into the water and allow it to drift like a Pooh stick under the bridge and off it goes down the stream towards the ocean. We touch on every topic, football, philosophy, politics, women and music. I know I must confront Ed about his actions towards Mick. I need to embolden myself. I need some courage. Tea! Yes, I've got the link!

'Tea?'

Ed nods. I make it down to the buffet car, but on the way I almost fall into the lap of a teenage girl. Her mother looks at me with a stare to dissolve the hardest of rocks. I feign a smile, mutter an apology and hurry on. On my return, the girl smiles at me and bats her eyelashes. I feign another smile and move even faster. She only looks about fourteen. I return to the table with two cups of piping hot tea. I place them on the table and give Ed his two portions of milk. We frantically open the containers and pour in the milk and stir.

'I wonder how many cups of tea we've enjoyed over the years?' I muse aloud.

'Hundreds, probably thousands.'

'D'you remember that pot of tea at the museum in China?'

'Which museum?'

'The National Tea Museum in Hangzhou.' Ed's face is still a blank. 'You know, where the girl served us fifteen different varieties and then concocted a special brew for us.'

'For everyone.'

'Don't be such a cynic! It was special! Not as special as the tea house in Moscow, now *that* I'll give you.'

Ed smiles a smile of recognition. Concealed in that smile are so many memories, funny moments, I know of many of those, but by no means all. I pause before I raise the subject.

'Clara was pleased to see you again.'

'I like your sister,' Ed adds matter-of-factly. He looks away and gazes out of the window. Ed seems to be staring into the distance, his eyes fixed on some point miles away, probably somewhere in the heart of Europe. The moment is lost.

THE HOUSE OF Soviets stands in the heart of Kaliningrad. It is the worst example of architecture to have ever been allowed to make the transition from the product of a deluded architect's brain to bricks and mortar. It has all the grace and charm of a Sixties car park. It seems an apt metaphor for the history of the Soviet Union. When it was built it was to be the central point of a new complex stretching out across the heart of the once proud Königsberg. It stands alone, unfinished, abandoned and ugly, a beautiful idea on paper; but in practice a monument to foolishness. Around the rim, new stalls are setting themselves up; the ubiquitous signs of American soft drinks manufacturers poke their heads proudly over the parapets.

It is the height of summer and yet the city seems drab and grey. The citizens of this once noble city shuffle along, their eyes fixed on the ground and not deflected by the buildings on either side. An old man, his dog in tow, hobbles along past the House of Soviets. He is singing to himself. I have to strain my ears in order to hear. It doesn't sound like a happy song, more of a lament. The dog is sniffing around, searching for something to chew, something to fill its stomach.

Ed is in his element. He is racing around. He is excited by a small plaque just to the side of the House of Soviets.

'Tom! Tom! Look!'

I move over towards my chum. His finger is out-stretched, pointing at a quotation inscribed on the plaque.

'What does it say?' He doesn't allow me time to answer before imploring me again, 'Come on, what does it mean? It's a quote from Kant! Look! What does it mean?'

I stare at the Russian lettering rather than the German translation. It reads, 'Two things fill the heart with ever a renewed and increasing awe and reverence, the more often and the more steadily we meditate upon them: the starry firmament above and the moral law within.' Ed joins me in the last three words, he knows this quote. It probably has been discussed at great length in one of his seminars.

He wanders around, a look of awe on his face. He clasps his hands to his chest, breathes in the dirty Kaliningrad air, closes his eyes and smiles a smile of sheer pleasure. One senses this is a momentous day in the life of Ed Bailey. All those hours stuck in his room ploughing through the great works of Western philosophy, all those hours of philosophy seminars, all those jokes levelled against him, all those hours invested into a quest to understand Königsberg's greatest citizen have been directed to such a moment.

Clara, Mick and myself do not share Ed's ecstasy, but at least we can benefit from the joy radiating from him. We may not have reached our Mecca, but we revel in the joy of someone who has reached his.

'TOM! ED!' THE order of names does not bode well for Ed's chances. Susi is running up the platform to meet us. She is wearing an orange cardigan and jeans. She has about five different necklaces bouncing up and down and hitting her chin as she speeds towards us; no doubt, all have been handcarved by some poor African tribesman. She flings her arms around my neck and kisses me on both cheeks very rapidly, before moving on to Ed where she performs the same action at an even more rapid pace. Ed thinks for a moment about putting his arms around the object of his desires, but decides against it; she would probably object. She escorts us to one of her 'favourite places'. Ed and I are ravenous after the long journey from the south. We gulp down the generous portions of curry, slurp the warm tea and begin to chat.

'So, um, how are the rehearsals going?' asks Ed.

He is leaning forward; his face is tilted to the right. He slowly wipes his lips with his napkin. I cannot hold back a smile.

'What are you smiling about?' asks Susi as she moves herself from a semi-recumbent posture to a bolt upright one. I try to suppress my smirk, but instead I burst out laughing. Ed looks across at me, rubs his chin with the side of his finger and frowns. Waves of animosity lap on to my shore. He must see me as the great obstacle. If only he knew how much I want to help him.

'Rehearsals are going *really* well.' Susi's voice stresses the 'really' a little too much. Ed would never dream of saying a harsh word, but I cannot resist.

'You're very confident. A little too confident.'

Susi leans over the table. She is a bellicose character at times, who loves to scrap over the tiniest of details. More correctly, she loves to win. She doesn't like the chase, just the kill. She looks at me; her beautiful blue eyes draw me in, her mouth twitches ever so slightly. I am hooked. She is hauling me in. I want her. I want her now. I want her here and now, on top of the table, in full view.

'Don't be so negative!' A voice shatters my thoughts. 'I'm sure they are going swimming,' adds the male voice. I turn my head and see Ed staring at me. The waves are higher than ever.

W E ARRIVED AT the party an hour ago. I still don't know whose party it is. Anybody who has the aura of a host is greeted with one of my nervous smiles. Across the room a pair of actors are discussing the intricacies of rolling a joint. One, with facial hair reminiscent of a sheepdog, is holding a piece of cigarette paper in his long fingers. He is moving the paper up and down, but cannot get a tight fit. The other is watching over him, the 'joint' police, checking everything is done well and properly. The talk is slow and inarticulate. Words are mumbled, except for the occasional 'yes' or the more common 'no!'

Ed is lying on the floor and staring at the ceiling, while talking to a tall man with thin vest and an armful of tattoos. I can't make out the topic of their conversation, the music is too loud. A podgy boy with bleached hair has been sitting by the stereo all evening. He has set up an exclusion zone around the CD player. Nobody, no matter who he or she is, is allowed in close proximity. Anyone who comes close will be fired upon by his glare. A beautiful South American girl suggested a little samba ten minutes ago but was refused point-blank.

I rise from the chair and proceed towards the kitchen. The route is littered with bodies sprawled out on the floor. The pungent aroma of freshly spilt alcohol fills the corridor. A girl with long brown hair and a pair of shiny black boots is holding her stomach as if someone is trying to steal it off her. I tiptoe through the bodies, carefully trying to avoid stepping on one of the poor souls.

The kitchen is full of people, lively people. It is always the hub of a good party. The hungry, the thirsty and the newly arrived tend to make their way straight to the land of fridges and well-stocked cupboards. Tonight is no exception. The fridge contains a fair selection of refreshment. Somebody has even dared leave a bottle of sparkling wine and a bottle of Russian vodka amongst the rows of cheap supermarket beer.

I find a bottle of German beer and look around for an opener. 'Has anyone seen the opener?' I enquire. Nobody responds. I repeat my request, this time with a little more volume, as I start to peer over the shoulders of those congregated in the kitchen. I put my hand on a shoulder, the nearest to hand, to give me some extra lift and a better view of the kitchen. A tall twenty-something with a bulbous nose and a huge red spot on his left cheek glowers at me. He rolls his shoulders and I almost detect his grunt. His anger is explicable. My left hand is placed on the shoulder of a frail girl with icy blue eyes, high cheekbones and shoulder-length brown hair. Her right is curled around his backside. I keep away from his prize and focus on the search. A helpful soul has started to aid me, informing me it was here a few moments ago.

I shrug my shoulders after three or four minutes of searching. I put the green bottle to my lips and yank the top off with my teeth. Howls of indignation can be heard throughout the kitchen. It is as if I had defecated on the kitchen floor.

The well-endowed girl turns to her protector and says indignantly 'Why did he do *that?*'

'Because I couldn't find the bottle opener,' I reply sarcastically.

Sometimes it is worth losing any chance with a pretty girl in order to deal with fatuity. Her protector steps forward, more out of a sense of obligation than a desire to pummel me into the ground. I take a swig of beer and leave the kitchen. She isn't worth it anyway.

The music has progressed from a steady stream of techno to cheesy Eighties pops. The blond boy has foresaken his exclusion zone for the chance to score with a pretty girl with large dark-brown eyes. He is animated and is throwing his arms around the room. I turn back towards the stereo. The music wolves are rooting through the CD collection desperately trying to find something cool. My eye wanders to the right, to a red dress. It's Susi. Susi is... My God! Susi is getting off with... with... Ed! I don't believe it! I have an urge to run up to them and congratulate Ed. He has been trying for so long. He's earned it. Fortunately I am not too drunk yet; I still have my faculties. Instead of lingering, I walk out of the room knowing my presence could spoil everything.

Fresh Scottish air is my only option. I have offended the kitchen and will annoy certain people if I remain in the front room. The option of the corridor with its pleasant aroma does not appeal. Fresh Scottish air, pure, clean and refreshing. Who said, 'All the best things in life are free'? It sounds fatuous, but what beats a dose of clean Scottish air? Maybe I should ask Ed and Susi.

I HAVE HAD to wait ten days, ten days to ask Ed what was the cause, the reason, the phrase, the *thing* that made Susi cross the Rubicon. Ed had not been evasive, but the moment had not been right. As Ed would have put it, it had not been propitious. We had been a threesome for most of the first few days. I had grown green and prickly and felt I was soon to be made into a fool. I had sat awkwardly as they embraced over coffee; I had stood as the third member of the party while we queued for the theatre; I had been a friend while Ed had been dragged in and smoothed with kisses. I felt envious. I wanted to have Susi. Now I wanted her, I couldn't have her. Perhaps I should tell Ed that Susi had thrown herself at me at my birthday party. She had picked up Ed in the reject shop.

How can I think such things about Ed? He is my best friend, a man whom I respect, a man who deserves some-one like Susi. He fought gallantly like a knight for her; he deserves his spurs. I, in contrast, haven't found what I'm looking for. Perhaps she is lurking around the next corner, perhaps not. Perhaps I found what I wanted in Prague, but I've lost Radka forever.

I am standing opposite the exit to Covent Garden tube. Pouring out of the ticket machines is a flood of women, a stream of the deepest blue, a stream of sheer delight; oh how I wish I could go for a dip, even a paddle.

Ed looks well. A beaming smile is emblazoned across his face. His right arm is thrusting itself towards me. Before I can react, he is shaking my right hand and patting my shoulder with his left.

'Good to see you!' he roars.

The whole of the street looks round. Ed is on cloud nine with roller skates.

'It's great to see you!'

I have never seen such a look on his face. I am dreading the conversation. I want to ask him about why Susi finally succumbed to his charm and why he had acted the way he did at the birthday party. Ed, no doubt, wants to talk about life with Susi. As we wander towards one of the cafés in Covent Garden, I want to avoid talking about Susi. Ed, fortunately, is clutching his copy of the *Guardian*. I ask him about the contents of the paper. He begins to recount a story about a woman aged fifty who has given birth to twins. I leap on to the topic. My false enthusiasm must show through. I am drivelling. Ed's face is turned away, he is watching the street performer swallow some fire. There is more than one mouth on fire.

'Two teas, please.'

'No, I think I'll have coffee.'

How can he drink coffee? Tea has always been the lubricant for our one-to-one chats. Susi's pernicious influence, I bet.

'I've got to thank you, mate. You were a great matchmaker, a wonderful lubricant; a fabulous love agent.' Ed pauses for dramatic effect. 'You don't charge for your services, do you?'

Another beaming smile, another joke. Does he really... Pull yourself together, Tom!

'I'm *really* pleased you two are together. I know you have tried to get together with dear old Susi for many years. Well done, mate!' My initial animosity was waning, reason was prevailing. Ed deserves Susi. She is bright, funny and sexy. He is warm, generous and charming. They deserve each other. I am so pleased I haven't said anything rash. To think I could have ruined it, deprived my best friend of a little happiness, by uttering a few callous remarks. Talk may be silver, but silence is sometimes golden. Sounds clichéd, but clichés are sometimes true.

'Do you mind me asking,' I enquire while leaning over the table towards him in a conspiratorial manner, 'what made her finally succumb to the legendary charm?'

'Alcohol.'

For all Ed's extensive vocabulary, his ability to wangle his way out of any difficult philosophical argument, at times he is brutally honest, a refreshing characteristic amongst those who chatter.

'Ed, can I ask you a question?' Ed nods assent. 'Sorry to be so direct, but I really must ask you. I know...' Stop labouring the point and spit it out! He is in a happy mood; his mood will probably never reach such heights again. 'Why did you leave my birthday party in such a rush? Moreover, why do you and Mick avoid each other?'

Ed's smile disappears. The waitress arrives with drinks. She makes up for Ed's expression. She smiles sweetly, places the drinks on the table and thanks us for thanking her. How terribly English! Ed picks up the sugar pot and pours some into the teaspoon. Something must be wrong, Ed doesn't drink coffee with sugar. He is silent. He half raises his head, but quickly brings it down again. I stir my pot of tea. The clink of metal and teapot seems loud. The silence seems deafening.

He begins to speak, but still refuses to lift his head. 'Basically,' he sighs, looking to his left and right, but his gaze returns to the pot of pure white sugar in front. 'Mick,' he says, stopping, sighing and continuing in a softer voice. barely audible, 'Mick thought I wanted to sleep with your sister and told me to stop leering at her.' He raises the volume slightly. 'Look nothing happened, all right. I wouldn't do that sort of thing. You know how I am usually reticent when it comes to women. Also, I know it sounds cruel, but I...' He looks away momentarily towards the counter and then fixes his glare on his coffee cup, lowering the volume control again says, 'I... don't fancy your sister and never have, she's...', he pauses, 'not that interesting.'

I know what Ed really means is Clara is not bright enough, she hasn't read any of the right books.

He raises his head and looks me straight in the eye. 'That's it, mate.' He adds, while his head droops a little more, 'Please can we not talk about it again?'

I look him in the eyes. Is it my imagination, or are there tears welling up inside Ed's eyes? He seems greatly affected by the topic of conversation. Why has his mood changed so rapidly from one of sheer ecstasy? Now is obviously not the time to probe.

'Thanks, mate, I really appreciate your candour.'

Part Three
Relative Values

WE ARE TOGETHER and yet all apart. Mick is in the land of nod, Clara is engrossed in a John Grisham thriller and Ed is reading the work of some obscure sixteenth-century German philosopher. Looking through the square window, I see a solitary cow. It must be bemused by the strange contraption which has come to a halt in the middle of its field.

The train has been stationary for fifteen minutes. Fifteen minutes to look at a rather unexceptional field in the middle of Lithuania. I know I wanted to see Lithuania, but not every blade of grass in this field. The others seem content to bury their heads in books and sleep; I feel restless. I rise from my seat and slip out the door. The other three don't seem to notice.

The corridor is full of people. A large man with a stained white vest and a beer belly is having an argument with an old lady. She is waving her walking stick at the man. They are speaking in Lithuanian, so I cannot understand anything, but the old lady is clearly upset by something. She keeps pointing at the man with her wooden stick, looking up at the sky and shaking her head. The large man just stands there saying little, just puffing away on a cigarette and periodically shrugging his shoulders. As I squeeze past them, some ash falls on my trouser leg. Instantly, the large man becomes animated. He shouts out something, I don't know the word, but from his intonation I deduce he must be apologising. He bends down to brush it off. Rather than running the risk of speaking Russian, I just utter a 'Thank you.'

'American?'

He points at me, nods his head repeatedly and smiles. I carry on the overacting.

'No! English!' I announce as I throw my head from side to side.

'English!'

The old woman joins in the round, her walking stick now firmly rooted to the spot.

I want to talk to these characters, whose gnarled faces probably have witnessed some fascinating events.

'*Vy gavaritye po Russky?*'

They nod. I apologise for using Russian, but they do not seem to mind.

'Where are you from in England?' asks the woman.

I understand the question, but cannot get past the solitary tooth left in her mouth. It is huge. She looks like a walrus.

'London.' Not strictly true, but who cares?

'I'm from Kaunas!' she announces with a big smile on her face. As she utters the place name, she looks around to see if anyone else can hear. She is proud of her home town.

'Do you know why the train has stopped?'

My two partners in conversation seem tickled by my accent, or is it my choice of words? I suddenly feel terribly self-conscious. The woman laughs, the man roars. Are they laughing at me? This is bloody rude. I begin to edge away, but am pulled back by a large hand grasping my arm. Is he going to mug me? Oh, my God! Should I hit him and run? Where to?

'The train will be here for some time! It's normal!'

Having a large sweaty hand on one's arm does not seem to be particularly normal to me. I turn round eager to face my tormentor. He greets my nervous face with a wide grin.

'Doesn't happen in London, eh?' he adds, removing his sweaty palm from my arm. He repeats the comment, stressing the 'doesn't'.

I smile more out of embarrassment than anything. I feel guilty for judging this character by a few well-meaning actions.

'Actually they are just as bad!'

He laughs at my response, but I can tell by the fact that he throws his head from side to side and fails to look me in the eye that he doesn't believe me.

'Do you know,' I add, 'one winter the train authorities blamed delays on the wrong kind of snow!'

Arms are thrown in the air, the single white tooth is displayed and the large sweaty hand pats me on the shoulder.

'The wrong kind of snow!'

His laughter becomes even louder. A head emerges from the next-door compartment. Its green eyes glare at our group. He can see our joviality and is probably envious. The jolly man wipes his sweaty hands on his vest and recounts the anecdote to the green eyes. They are amused. The eyes belong to a tall thin man. He is dressed in a corduroy jacket and jeans. A thin green tie made of some cheap and nasty material adorns his chest.

'Are you from London?' asks the man in a beautiful, crisp Oxford accent, the English words tripping off his tongue with ease and velocity.

I nod and reply, 'Yes, I study there.'

The man nods. I think for a moment, but cannot stop myself from asking a clichéd follow-on. 'Have you ever been to London?' I point rather stupidly at him. Why did I point at him? It is obvious I am talking to him.

'Yes. I spoke at a conference last year.'

'On what?'

'Astrophysics.'

The two others in the group are staring at the man with disbelief. Their boisterous behaviour seems to have subsided. Their sidelong looks make me feel rather nervous. The use of my vernacular is isolating them from the conversation. I try to rescue the conversation by shifting topic and language.

'I wonder how long we will be here?'

'Ages,' says the tooth.

'Not too long,' says the stained vest.

'Maybe it's the wrong kind of sunlight!' jokes the green eyes.

Laughter ensues. The sweaty palm pats my back again. The tooth displays itself to all who care to look. The carriage door opens. A ticket inspector in his thirties with three-day stubble struts purposefully towards the group of happy travellers. He says something quickly in Lithuanian; the other three raise their eyebrows. The tooth, the green eyes and the sweaty palm begin to ask questions. The designer stubble points at his watch, shrugs his shoulders, points out of the window and walks off. I can see people walking from the train. This isn't a station. Has the train broken down?

'Do you swim?' asks the green eyes, his accent even more Oxonian than before. Is he expecting me to swim to Kaunas?

The large man fiddles around in his bag and pulls out a towel. He rolls it up carefully and methodically and shouts, 'Let's go!'

I am baffled. We are supposed to be travelling to Kaunas. We should be there in ten minutes, we are well behind schedule and the rest of the train has decided to go swimming. Is the world going mad? My friendly astrophysics professor smiles, slaps me on the back and informs me, with an animated grin on his face, 'The conductor says the train will be here for an hour, maybe two. Down there', he says, pointing out of the window, 'is a lake. Do you want to come swimming?'

I'm incredulous and my sentences are short.

'Swimming? Now?'

The other three seem keen for me to join them. I stop. Should I go? What if the train leaves without me? Stranded with only my swimming trunks and a towel. Is this wise?

'Just a moment.'

I run back towards our compartment; the conductor is still in view. I run up to the man. I apologise for speaking Russian; I tell him my ethnic origin.

'The train will be here for a long time?'

He nods.

'If we go swimming down there, you will wait for us, please?'

He nods and smiles.

'I am going to get my towel,' he announces, a broad grin across his face. 'You wait here. We go down together and, when I come back, I tell you. Okay!'

He has reassured me.

'I'm going swimming!' I announce as I enter our compartment.

Clara looks up; she has managed to drag herself away from Grisham. She looks at me, disbelief across her face. She remains silent for a preposterously long period of time, then she stumbles out a reply.

'W... W... What did you? Swimming? But we're on a... train!'

'The train's going to be here for hours. Do you want to come?'

I am animated. The rest of my group does not seem taken by this suggestion. Clara looks at me as if I have suggested an evening with Adolf Hitler.

'I'll stay here and look after the stuff.' declares Ed. 'I'm engrossed in my book. I don't want to stop.'

If anyone other than Ed said such a thing I would doubt their sincerity, but Ed has been reading the book all day. Every five minutes he has scribbled something in the margin. He would prefer to swim another few miles of his philosophical voyage than paddle about with some Lithuanians. Fair enough.

'Mick, do you want to come swimming?'

'Can't afford it.'

'In the lake down there,' I point vaguely in the right direction.

He looks at the end of my finger, rather than in the direction I'm pointing, just like a pet. His head moves from side to side. He leans back, rests his head against the headrest and closes his eyes to the world of possibility.

I FEEL SO excited, like a little boy. My heart is pounding, my knees are trembling. Cliché, cliché. I haven't been on a date for ages, not for months, not for years. The last chronological period is true, but I couldn't admit it to my friends. Pride.

I have planned it well, I think. Time, as Mick would say, is on my side. I check my watch again, just in case. Just in case of what? I checked the damn thing only a minute ago. It isn't going to be anything serious, just a date.

Lucy. Lucy. I met her in a café in central London. She was there with Vlad the Mad, or Derek, as he was known to all outside the Russian class. She was engaging, witty and charming. She wasn't that beautiful, or was she? My memory of her now seems so hazy. I cannot even remember her face. No, I exaggerate, but that meeting seems so long ago.

I remember Ed telling me about his date with Susi last week. He was nervous, worried that, without the captivating Edinburgh air, she would find him dull, boring, or just tiresome, as she was wont to do. He had thought about buying new glasses that morning, but on grounds of cost decided against it. On the way, as he became engrossed in some obscure thirteenth-century philosopher's greatest work, he adjusted the positioning of his glasses. Out it popped! How embarrassing! There it was in his lap and all the beady eyes were watching. His right lens had fallen from the frame. He took off the glasses, squinted and attempted to fathom out the cause. A tiny right-hand screw had come loose. He placed the lens back into the frame and tried to tighten up the lens with his fingernail. The screw, however, fell from the frame on to the floor. Ed squinted. He felt around on the floor for the screw. Eventually he found it. Picking up the screw, however, was a different matter. He dropped it not once, not twice, but five times more. Eventually he picked up the screw, managed to hold on to it and placed it in his palm. Ed, with the assistance of a London Underground assistant's screwdriver, managed to secure the lens in place. You can rely on the Tube.

Lucy is standing outside the film theatre when I arrive. The first part of my plan has gone to pot. Surely the gentleman should be there before the lady. A lady shouldn't have to wait alone. Enough of chivalry, I think. You just have to make do with whatever you've got.

She looks attractive, tall with long, blond, flowing locks, blue eyes to boot and a pair of wonderful legs. And yet, she has so many bad points. Her preponderance for elaborate make-up, a loud laugh and, most disturbingly of all, she is reading the *Daily Telegraph*. Most men can justify reading the 'Torygraph' because it has excellent sports coverage, but I hope she doesn't shelter reactionary views. To give her her due she is prepared to come and watch a bizarre Russian film with me. She must be game for a laugh. Besides, Mr Kelly, my old history teacher, read the *Telegraph* and he was one of the soundest men I've ever met. Don't, I implore myself, be too negative.

How should I greet her? A handshake seems far too formal, too distant, too aloof. A kiss on the cheeks *à la française*? A bit too Continental or false. Um… I don't have any more time. Desperate to know what, to do, I launch into my bear-hug. I'm seeking comfort from my troubles.

She squeals out a 'Hi!' I tell my subconscious to go forth and multiply.

That one stupid act, one folly, has caused me to look so stupid. Lucy starts to engage in small talk. I respond with small talk. We are both stuck in first gear without a gearstick. That first moment, that first chance, to make a difference has disappeared. I struggle to extricate myself from the mistake, but both of us seem to know that that simple almost insignificant act has determined our relationship for ever. The rest of the evening is pleasant enough, but a single solitary moment of madness has ended all chances of attaining the heights we had both hoped for.

CLARA IS IN London for the day. We have met for some refreshment in a café in Islington run by a pair of amiable Turks. They try to coax us into consuming some of their elegantly prepared food, but we are content to consume coffees and teas.

Clara is fiddling with her spoon, dipping it into the sugar bowl and stirring it around and around. Grains of white fall over the side of the container on to the table. She looks around to see if anyone noticed. By turning around she only serves to advertise the fact that something has happened. One of the waiters, dressed in a long blue apron, emblazoned with a map of the homeland, begins to advance towards the table. I sense Clara's embarrassed face staring down towards the table. I feel I should do something gallant. I take the easy option. 'Another tea and another coffee, please.' The waiter changes direction. Crisis averted. Very Chekhovian.

'I've got some news for you,' Clara announces as she continues to stir the sugar. Don't some people ever learn? 'Mick asked me to marry him, yesterday.'

'Really?' I muse. What a stupid answer. An exclamation, a smile, even an 'Oh, my God!' would have been better than a 'really'. It sounds like I don't care.

'I said, "Yes".' She smiles as the word emanates from her orifice. Before I can say anything, she thrusts her hand into my face. 'Isn't it beautiful?' she says.

'Yes, wonderful.'

I hadn't even noticed the diamond on her finger all afternoon. Perhaps I need my eyes tested, perhaps I'm still thinking about that evening with Lucy. 'Have you named the day?' I add, desperate to sound at least a little enthusiastic.

'You don't sound very happy! What's the matter? Hey! Mick's a wonderful guy! Aren't you pleased? The first bit of exciting news for ages in my fucking life and you have to fucking spoil it. Thanks a lot! Fuck off!'

Clara stands up, jogs the waiter, spills the coffee and storms out of the café.

'Clara! Clara! What's the…'

She's gone. I slump back into my chair. Eyes, beady eyes are staring at me. I feel so stupid. I try to maintain my dignity, but after a couple of minutes of the beady eyes, I pay up and leave.

I find solace in a second-hand bookshop just south of the tube station. I find an Eco in the corner and make my way to the cash desk. My eye is caught by a thin book lying on top of a pile. It is a copy of Albert Camus's *The Fall*. I read it years ago, but now seems the right time to buy the novel. I, too, like Meursault, am refusing to follow the conventions of society. It is clearly a rule to congratulate your sister on her proposed wedding, even if you think it a mistake.

'S HE'S WHAT!'
'Will you let me finish the anecdote?'
'Your sister's getting married to Mick?'
'Yes. Now let me finish the anecdote, please.'

Ed, however, does not seem interested in hearing my account of the incident. Or indeed the bit about Camus which he would surely appreciate. I sense something is wrong. My birthday party and again now, here. Why?

'What's up?'

'Nothing!'

'What have you got against Mick?' I ask, leaning forward, my eyes fixed on his face.

'Nowt.'

'Come on, Ed, at my birthday you avoided him like the plague and now you seem distressed because he's marrying my sister.' I pause for a second. 'Do you fancy my sister?'

'Don't you start! Can we change the subject? If not, I'd like to go home, or go and see Susi, my *girlfriend*!' He glances at his watch. Without giving me a chance to change the subject, he adds, 'Look it's late, I'm going home, okay?' Ed gets up quickly and walks off.

I sit in the café for a while, just staring at the table. What have I done wrong? What's wrong with me? I have upset both my best friend and sister in consecutive days. I wonder what I should do. I order another tea and begin to read and read. I finish off the rest of the novel. Maybe I'll find my day when I can blow my trumpet.

My mind is lifted as I close the back cover. It begins to wander back to what Ed said. 'Don't *you* start.' It seems a strange choice of words. It suggests someone else had started to have a go at him. Perhaps Susi had argued with him. Perhaps his mum had berated him for something. I pay the bill and wander down to the nearest phone. Susi's line isn't engaged, but it rings and rings and rings. Eventually someone answers.

'Hello. It's Tom!'

'Hi!' She sounds happy. No hint of an argument.

'Sorry to ask a personal question, but I've just spoken to Ed and he seems... well...' I pause, I've got to use the right word. 'He seems a little upset. I wondered whether...'

'No, everything's fine between us.' Susi's brain is alive to my train of thought. She adds, 'He was on top of the world this morning.'

My smutty little brain wants to say...

'Yes, Tom, he *was* on top of me as well this morning!' she bellows down the phone. I can't believe she just said that!

After exchanging a few pleasantries and recounting my anecdote about Camus we end our conversation, my mind still no nearer the cause of Ed's annoyance. Perhaps Ed is upset with Susi. She can sometimes upset other people's sensibilities without realising it. Her last comment was an example of that. I sit on a bench for a while. It really bugs me. I want to be a fine political journalist, uncovering all those interesting stories and I can't even fathom out why my best friend is upset. How the hell am I going to understand the motives of politicians?

That journey. That journey holds the key. Something must have happened, but what? It must have been significant. But what?

ED AND I are sitting in the bus station. Our bus leaves in one hour's time, but we are ready to move on. Not that we haven't enjoyed the delights of Vilnius, capital of Lithuania, but an evening of jazz has taken its toll. We are both shattered. Ed is leaning back to rest his head on the pile of rucksacks. The sun is setting, but it is generously providing the citizens of this capital city with a warm summer evening and a stunning sunset.

Clara approaches. She smiles at me as our eyes meet. She is clutching a large loaf of bread under her left arm, leaving the right to swing with her steps. She looks tired. Three weeks of travel, three weeks of irregular sleep, three weeks of Ed, Mick and me. Mick is following behind, his hands full with huge sausages and a bag of fruit.

Ed leaps up from his recumbent position and rushes towards Clara and exclaims, 'My saviour! My saviour!' in a loud quasi-Russian accent. 'Thank you! Oh, Great One! Thank you!' he adds in grovelling tones. He takes Clara's hand, bows his head and kisses her like a French courtier. Laughter ensues, smiles all around. Clara's face doesn't need any blusher. She looks from side to side, smiles again and pats Ed on his head. Her hand lingers for a second as if she were anointing him.

The bus draws up to the stop ready for loading. One lady seems to have five carrier bags full of cigarettes, another has plenty of bottles full of a clear liquid. It is too tempting, I tell myself, to consider they are vodka. Maybe they are water, or lemonade, or... My mind desperately tries to find a third colourless liquid to finish off the troika, but my brain isn't functioning at the moment.

Mick is standing by the timetable, nonchalantly biting into his roll. He seems distant and unenthralled by the next stage of our journey. Clara walks up to him, puts her hand on his shoulder and rests her head up against his arm. Seconds tick away, then he turns his head towards the lady on his arm, he whispers something and they embrace.

Should I break up this romantic moment? I wonder for a second whether I ought to. The bus is loading, we will soon be departing, tickets have been bought, plans made. What about spontaneity? We are on holiday after all; we don't have to follow some pre-arranged plan. Ed would probably say we must follow the categorical imperative, but then he would, wouldn't he? I just wanna have a good time! What a profound dilemma.

The embrace ends before it is resolved. Circumstances can sometimes sort out these things. They turn towards me, clasping each other's hands and wander down to our pile of rucksacks. A beautiful romantic scene. My eye, however, is caught by a tall elegant woman who is now standing by the timetable. She has such a lot upfront. I berate myself for slipping from philosophy to smut so quickly.

'She's a bit of all right, ain't she?' comes a voice over my shoulder. 'I'd give her one! Still we gotta go! The travails of modern life, eh.'

Great minds think alike, or is it just that small minds rarely differ?

The bus has uncomfortable seats, dirty seat covers and no air-conditioning. It does, however, have a video. I sometimes wonder about other people's sense of priorities.

The TV is beaming out Rod Stewart strutting his stuff on stage. The other passengers do not seem to be enthralled. Two women are having a lively discussion at the front of the bus. Fingers are pointing, voices raised. An elderly man replete with walking stick and cigarette is standing to the side staring at the two combatants. He interjects. His words, in Lithuanian, are beyond my comprehension. The women turn their heads and glower at the man. Waves of animosity flow from both women. They are having a private argument. Nobody else is allowed to join in. The old man turns away and returns to his seat.

*

We have been waiting in this queue for nearly two hours. The queue is stationary. No prospect of movement seems to be on the horizon. We had been making good progress. We had been pelting along the highways of Lithuania without any major hitches, but as the Lithuanian-Polish border approached, we had begun to slow to halt.

Clara rouses from the land of nod. She wipes her hand with the back of her hand and looks from side to side. Her right arm is used to lift herself from her semi-recumbent posture. Her eyes catch mine, the corners of her mouth turn upwards.

'Where are we?'

'At the border,' I reply. 'We've been here for nearly two hours.'

'Have you been counting?' Clara responds sarcastically.

I look at her for a moment and wonder how someone can be so sarcastic so soon after being raised from sleep. I put on a false smile and look away.

The driver, a short man with a fiery red shirt and a preponderance of nasal hair, is wandering up the aisle with what seems to be a green bucket. The fellow travellers seem to be placing money in it. To our right is a kiosk, advertising beer. Perhaps he is going on a delivery run. He approaches the four of us, a broad grin plastered on his face. He says something in Lithuanian. I ask him in Russian for three beers and a Coke. He smiles, wags his little finger and repeats his request. He is more animated now. He stresses every vowel and raises the volume, probably thinking that by so doing the complexities of the Lithuanian language will be revealed to us.

It suddenly dawns. It is a bribe to ease our way. Should we pay? As a child I was always taught never to pay someone who demands money, they just come back for more. I pretend to be utterly baffled by his request. He asks again.

'English! English!' I retort, waving my passport at him.

He signals his defeat and retreat by sighing, shaking his head, turning away and swiping his right arm from right to left.

I watch him as he gets off the bus and, in full view of everyone, passes over the bucket to an official who is wearing a thick woollen coat and a hat which looks as if it has swallowed a large plate. The official examines the contents, nods and within a minute the engine has been revved up and we are on our way.

'Why did the driver come round with the bucket?' asks Ed, as the bus pulls away from its temporary stop.

'He was collecting money.'

'Why?'

'To bribe the border official,' I answer matter-of-factly.

'We *bribed* a border official?' perks up Clara. 'What... but... Shit!... Why?' she adds eloquently.

'We can't afford to do that,' adds Mick.

'I read', responds Ed, 'in *Vilnius In Your Pocket* that some cars have to wait up to six days at the border. If we hadn't greased someone's palm, we'd be here for days!'

'But that's totally outrageous!' Clara is appalled. 'What would your bloody moral philosophers say about that?' She stares at Ed. She thinks she has hit the jackpot.

'A necessary sacrifice on the road to the building of the New Jerusalem,' Ed responds, his verbal boxing gloves having been donned.

Clara refuses to rise to the challenge, shakes her head and closes her eyes.

L AST WEEK I arranged to meet Ed today to see an exhibition at the Royal Academy. My mind traverses the ground of recent days. Yesterday, he seemed so upset. I feel full of remorse. Ed is my best friend, a true soulmate. Why did I probe him yesterday? He had given me a straight answer that afternoon in Covent Garden, why did I probe further? Shouldn't one trust one's best friend? He gave me a straight answer, I should accept that as the truth.

I am not satisfied. There still seem to be unresolved questions. Ed has something against Mick. Whenever the two of them meet there is a palpable tension. Why? Does my sister hold the key? Or, perhaps, Clara is just the symptom rather than the cause.

A small child catches my eye. He has a pair of glasses perched on the edge of his nose. They look as if they are going to drop off and crash on to the floor. He is being dragged, kicking and screaming, by his mother into the gallery. There is a snapping sound. The glasses lie twisted on the tarmac. The mother is shouting and screaming at the little boy.

'Why did you do that you, stupid boy! I can't take you anywhere!' I hope that isn't a portent.

I glance at my watch. Ten thirty. He is late, not an understandable ten or just about excusable fifteen minutes, but half an hour. Should I stay or should I go? It's so unbelievable! Ed is usually so reliable. I feel I ought to wait. Delays sometimes do occur. I begin to pace like a pregnant father, periodically glancing at my watch. Seconds tick by, but still no sign of my chum, my pal. I feel such a fool. My big mouth. If I had kept it shut none of these problems would have emerged. Yet, I still feel there is something I should know, something there, some dark secret that has been kept from me. I feel like a deprived child.

Eleven o'clock and still no sign of Ed. I decide to stop brooding and to stop waiting. I walk up the steps, pay my money to the woman behind the cash desk and walk up the elegant staircase. Monet draws me in. Bridges, bridges and bridges. How apt!

I arrive home uplifted by my visit and yet guilt still haunts me. I feel I have acted in a terribly selfish way. I feel fingers are pointing at me. Guilty! Guilty! You caused your friendship to break up. You caused your best friend to storm out of a café. You upset your sister. You are an evil insidious character! Evil!

The green light of the answering machine is flashing. I press the button nonchalantly while taking off my jacket.

'This is a message for Emma. Hi, it's David. Hope you enjoyed last night. Maybe we can get together again soon.' Bleep.

'Emma. It's Sam. Love to see you soon, please give me a call.' Bleep.

'Tom. It's Dad. Give me a call sometime today. I've got some news to tell you.' Another bleep.

'Tom, it's Ed.'

I stop in mid-flow; my jacket is off one arm, but not the other.

'Look, there's a problem with the washing machine at home, it's leaking all over the floor. I'm gonna have to stay here. Sorry I can't make it to the exhibition. Hope you get the message before you leave. Take care and give me a call later on today.'

I throw my head back, stare at the ceiling and emit all the air from my lungs. I feel relieved. Obviously Ed's anger has disappeared, or at least died down. Thank you, God.

M UM HAS INVITED Clara and me to Sunday lunch. The four of us have not sat down for a meal together for a long time. We had all been in the house at the same time during my birthday party, but we hadn't sat down and put the world to rights.

I spent this morning wandering down the local High Street. It is strange, but every holiday, every time I return to the shops of my youth, I feel more and more of a stranger. The shops are timeless. They have an air of permanence. Even though the local electrical store has a sign advertising new CD players, new washing machines, new televisions, everything seems just as I left it. Admittedly, Mr Sainsbury has opened a new store, but that doesn't feel new, just catching up with the present.

The local second-hand bookshop at the top of the High Street still has the mordant, cantankerous man behind the counter. How can a man, surrounded by a wealth of fascinating books, a man who always has Radio Four or jazz playing away on his stereo, be so miserable? Perhaps it is just me. Perhaps he is thinking it is that bloody student who tries to off load all his third-rate novels and turgid textbooks every time he enters. This time, however, I come with bulging pocket.

In his back room, where he can only spy on customers through his camera lens, I feel more relaxed. I feel more at ease knowing the camera rather than the man is watching me. I always feel as if I am going to steal something in the front room. His eyes tell me I am guilty, guilty of being, guilty, guilty.

My eye settles on 'K'. I pick out the first novel and begin to read the first few pages. The author begins to talk about Nietzsche's theory of eternal recurrence. Does that mean I have to live through that evening with Rebecca Fry again. Everything had been going so well. I had bought some flowers and tickets for a classical music concert. I had even told her who the chamber orchestra was going to be. Had she told me her *friend*, Natasha, was going to be there playing first violin? No! Had she told me they were once lovers? No! I just found out at the end of the first half when Rebecca walked up to the front, clambered on the stage and started to kiss Natasha. Lesbianism is still shocking to the suburbs. The rest of the audience spent the remainder of the evening staring at Rebecca and me, staring at us. The opprobrium of the good citizens of my town was directed at us for the rest of the evening. I have nothing against two women kissing, but it made me look as if I had either been duped by Rebecca or I was prepared to play second fiddle while she waited for the first. Pride will always be more important than prejudice.

I find another book, written by another dissident and entitled *My First Loves.* I emit one of those noises of recognition. Air comes out of the nose and the head rolls back. Another customer hears me and looks in my direction. I take my handkerchief from my pocket and wipe my nose. Pride again? No, just a desperate desire to conform. I read the first few pages of the book and resolve to buy it. I am entranced by the description of the small boy falling in love under the Nazis. Maybe the poets are fight, maybe love conquers everything!

I feel a tap on the shoulder.

'I thought I might find you here!' exclaims a female voice.

It is Clara, wearing something very strange. It is not quite a dress and not quite, well, I don't know. She seems elated. Standing next to her is Mick. He smiles and grasps Clara's shoulder. I smile. There is a pause. A long pause. Clara is looking at me. She nods slightly as if she is prompting me. Revelation!

'Congratulations!' I take Mick's hand and shake it firmly, 'You must be so happy!' I pause for a second and then add apologetically, 'You'll have to forgive me, I was miles away. You know me and bookshops.'

Mick smiles a smile of recognition. He knows I can get absorbed by these dens of iniquity. The excuse is therefore at least plausible.

'We'll leave you in peace,' declares Clara. She knows I want to spend my morning in bookshops, lunchtime and beyond will be the time for family discussions. My sister sometimes does the right thing.

My journey from 'K' back to the cash desk is fraught with difficulties. I feel trapped by the forces around me. A book on Prague castle to my left, a book on beetles to my right. My eyes cannot avoid a few gems glaring at me. Tolstoy's masterpieces stare at me from the 'T' shelf. I cannot resist picking them up, looking at the prices and putting them down. Why? I have both books, I have read both books. I would pay fifty pounds, no, a hundred pounds, for each. Why am I so intrigued by the price the mordant bookseller has scribbled into the book with his blunt HB pencil? Some bizarre, perverse desire to see whether I had bought the book more cheaply. I appal myself sometimes with my triviality.

The shopkeeper sighs as I pass over the money. No doubt too much effort. After I thank him, he manages to raise a smile, but he doesn't remove his hand from his left cheek. It has found a happy home within his beard and it doesn't want to move. I resolve never to go into the shop again. If he doesn't want my business, I'll go elsewhere. In this small town, however, he has no competition. He can do whatever he chooses. So much for freedom.

Clara and Mick are already drinking a glass of wine by the time I arrive home. Dad has bought some special wine, winner of some award or other. He seems pleased. Mick is wearing one of his figure-hugging T-shirts again, displaying his masculinity. Clara seems pleased.

After lunch, Mick makes his excuses and leaves. Mum and Dad decide to go for a walk. I am left with Clara.

'I'm sorry I was so short with you, the other day.'

'Don't worry about it. I should have been at least a tad more enthusiastic.'

I am genuine in my admission of guilt, but why do humans have this tendency to argue with horrible vocabulary and then make up amicably later? It all seems terribly irrational and a waste of energy.

'I know you're not that big a fan of Mick, but I want you to know I do genuinely love him. He', she pauses, clears her throat and then adds, 'is the man for me!' She looks down at the carpet and then looks me straight in the eye. 'Why don't you like Mick?' The tone of her voice has changed to that of an inquisitor. 'What's wrong with him?'

I hesitate. My inquiring mind wants to know the answers to some questions. Should I ask them? Today seems to be a day to spit it out.

'Why does Ed hate Mick?'

'He doesn't.' A curt answer revealing nothing. She looks back into my eyes and repeats her original question. She thrusts her head forward, she wants to know why.

'Look...' I rise from the sofa, put my hands into my trouser pockets, rock back on my heels and add, 'I think Mick is an okay bloke. He's not exactly my cup of tea, but then I don't expect my sister to pick her boyfriends on the basis of what her brother thinks.'

Clara is still frowning at me. She isn't satisfied by my perfectly reasonable answer. I ponder for a second. Should I go in for the kill? Should I risk it? If I want to be a top journalist I've got to ask awkward questions.

'Ed is my best friend, I value his opinion. Before we went on that journey, he thought Mick was okay, nothing special, admittedly, but okay. He hadn't seen Mick for two years after that journey and yet, at my birthday party, he avoided him like the plague. Why?'

Clara rises from the sofa. She turns towards the window. The rain is beginning to pour. Puddles of water are collecting on the drive. Clara stretches out her hand to touch the window frame. Her index finger touches first, then she spreads her other fingers across the pane. Her head droops slightly. She turns back towards me.

'Look. I know something must have happened between them, but I don't know what. All I know is that Mick thought Ed was trying it on with me. He wasn't. Mick knows that.'

'Did anything happen? Was there a big argument?'

'I... I never saw one. They never seemed to argue in front of my face. Of course, it could have happened behind my back, but I don't, I... I don't know.'

'Do you suspect anything happened?'

The truth seems close, I can smell it. The bottom of this mystery is near.

'Something might have happened on the train between Budapest and Paris. You had already left for Berlin or Prague or wherever you went. Ed got out of the train in Vienna. It seemed like a sudden decision, but Ed wanted to eat cake or something. We shook hands with Ed and then wished each other a *bon voyage* and that was that. After that we went on to France and had such a wild time. For those few days in the sun, money didn't seem to be an object. It was wonderful by the beach. The only drawback was Mick was under doctor's orders not to go swimming.'

Clara shrugs her shoulders. She seems baffled. She is not alone.

Part Four
Of That Crooked Timber

I START WORK tomorrow. My student days are finally over. The days of long summer holidays, of cheap beer, of late starts and early finishes, have gone. Tomorrow I must don suit and tie and join the massed ranks of the working population.

I allow myself one day of indulgence on my last day of freedom. Even though I wake at nine, I lie in bed until eleven thirty. My mind flicks through memories. Half-forgotten words, embarrassing actions, happy moments are recalled in chaotic fashion. I stare at the ceiling and smile. My life has taken a happy trajectory, simple, direct, success-ful. A warm glow envelops my soul.

I decide to treat myself to an all-day English breakfast in a greasy spoon in south London. Tucked away in the heart of the pink shopping centre, I find a suitable eatery. I sit in the corner. The waitress approaches. She has a cheerful expression and asks, with a hint of a foreign accent, what I want. I glance at the menu and turn my head back to the waitress. My eye is caught by a large tattoo on her right forearm. On closer inspection, it is a knife with a snake wrapped around it.

'Sausage, egg, chips and beans, please.'

She scribbles something down on her notepad.

'And a tea,' I add before she has a chance to ask whether I require anything to wash my meal down with.

She returns in quick time laden with my request. I cannot get that excited by the food and I cannot take my eyes of the tattoo.

After polishing off my plateful of protein, carbohydrate and fat, I make my way to the tube station. In the subway, a bedraggled character is slumped against the wall, a large brown blanket his only source of comfort. A dirty McDonald's cup in front of him contains a few measly pence. He looks into my eyes. Depression, hunger, cold, failure look at me. His eyes carry no anger. They do not seem to have the energy to be angry, they are too enervated. I reach into my pocket and find a pound coin. Tomorrow I will be earning one of these every five minutes. Every five minutes, this person, this other member of the human race, will be sitting here getting cold, hungry and depressed. I place a coin in the cup and begin to walk off.

I feel pleased by my act of supererogation. 'Look at me! Aren't I good!' I feel like saying. I am falling down the chute.

I take the tube to Charing Cross. I emerge by Trafalgar Square. Pigeons are flying everywhere. Tourists are throwing bird seed into the air, it is raining down all over the road. A small demonstration is taking place in the square. A hundred people are standing on the north side of Nelson's Column. A collection of microphones has been erected beside one of the lions. An Asian man is shouting into one of the microphones, but his accent is too strong. I cannot understand a word of what he is saying. I decide not to linger.

Leicester Square is full of tourists. A group of Italian students, decked out with identical rucksacks, munching away on their hamburgers and marching in time to the command of their group leader, make their way through the square. To their left a drunk is ferreting among the litter bins, his gnarled face not one which would grace a postcard. Ahead a group of Bolivians or Peruvians are playing away on their pan pipes. A large crowd has gathered around. Feet are tapping, heads are nodding, money is being thrown into the pot.

I wander through the square and on towards Eros. Clustered around the statue are tourists from all four corners of the globe. Two Japanese girls are studying a map. Behind them a Canadian, proudly displaying a maple leaf on his rucksack, is gazing up at the sky and taking a hugely enjoyable drag from his cigarette. Two Mediterranean girls are sitting to the Canadian's right; they are obviously interested in him. I can hear the giggles from twenty metres away.

St James's Park is virtually empty. Not even the vibrant colours of the flowers can compensate for the lack of people. A solitary bespectacled man clad in a dark pin-striped suit is sitting on one of the benches. He is sporting a red rose in his left lapel, a black attaché case to his right. He is reading a copy of the *Daily Telegraph*. He looks like a character out of a Le Carré novel. My eyes linger a second too long. The gent raises his eyes over his gold-rimmed, half-moon glasses and stares at me. His look is penetrating. I wonder whether he thinks I work for the other side. Probably not, I am just a nosy nobody. I cannot spy anyone else nearby, only a small Indian boy running around screaming.

Buckingham Palace looks suitably regal today. From the top of the building a single flag, a solitary Royal Standard, flies, high, mighty and omnipotent. Liz is at home. I wonder whether she is sitting watching afternoon TV? Perhaps she is dabbling in a light afternoon dusting or cooking Phil a kebab and chips? My mind is tickled by the thought that the monarch might be doing something as exciting as the rest of her subjects. Maybe not.

Ed has agreed to meet me today. He wanted to spend the evening drinking, but I want to be on top form for work, so we compromise on one early evening beer. We have agreed to meet at a bar in Clapham, one of Ed's favourites. It is full of bright, articulate, intellectual types, but from the right side of the barricades. The pub is owned by a workers' co-operative, the profits siphoned off to a host of good causes, strikers, Cuba and suchlike. Ed is in his element. He wants to persuade me to keep up the good fight. He is genuinely pleased I have landed a great job, but he'd prefer it if I were writing for a left-wing paper, not the house journal of the City, the *Financial Times*.

'Looking forward to tomorrow?'

'Yeah, but I've got the usual nerves. You know.'

'I can't believe you are going to be wearing a suit and tie. You'll be a bloody taxpayer tomorrow. You'll start voting Conservative soon!' Ed smiles mischievously, while delivering the last comment.

He looks well. He seems happy with his life. He was always destined to remain at university all his life. I try to imagine Ed working in a factory. He would start a riot, not because he is a great troublemaker, but he would be so bored he would need to liven up the proceedings as the goods trundled along the conveyer belt. 'Power to the people!' or more aptly, 'Power to those who have read all the great left-wing thinkers and want to do something to improve the workers' lot. Power to all those who have gold-rimmed Lennon specs! Yeah!'

Ed once told me about a riot he helped start during his schooldays, during a woodwork class – just imagine Ed in a woodwork class! Having to work like a worker! There was a boy called Peter Potter who had spent the first ten years of his life in some South American country, in consequence he wasn't white like the rest of the boys. The woodwork teacher was an old die-hard fascist, Mr Dickson, the type of man who ends up in an all-boys' school teaching wood-work. He was something in the war, he always told the class. It was discovered he had only been a hospital porter, which actually meant he rose in Ed's estimations, as if Mr Dickson, or 'Tapper' as the class used to call him due to his lack of hair on top, was a proto-Wittgenstein. Only Ed would make a link like that. Only Ed.

One afternoon, Potter arrived late to the class. Mr Dick-son rubbed his hands on his dirty apron and reluctantly let the diminutive boy into the workshop.

'Afternoon, Tapper, sir,' said Potter.

The remainder of the class laughed. Mr Dickson looked around. He knew he had to show the unruly mob who was boss. He wiped his hands on his dirty apron again, as if that was going to make them any cleaner, and walked up to Potter.

'Boy! I've told you once and I'll tell you again. You call me Mr Dickson! Right!'

'Yes, Mr Cockson!'

'The name, boy, is Dickson, you little twerp! I did not fight in the war to have people like you talk to me like that!'

'You didn't fight in the war, Tapper! You were just a hospital porter!'

Potter laughed and laughed and laughed. He picked up a lump of wood and began to wave it at the symbol of authority. The flies that had collected on the plank were disturbed.

'Mr Tapper is a twat!'

'I've had enough of you, you little nigger!'

With that Mr Dickson thrust his rotund body into motion and lunged towards Potter.

Potter began to run around the workstation, waving his plank of wood and shouting at the top of his voice, 'Come and get me, twat!'

Ed was roused from his slumber. He usually found the double period of woodwork to be deeply soporific. He took a piece of wood from the table and started to shout, 'Rhubarb! Rhubarb!' The timid and the brave amongst his woodwork class began to join in. Potter continued to run. Dickson tried to catch him, but the class continued to obstruct their teacher. And all this to the accompaniment of a chorus of 'Rhubarb! Rhubarb!' Potter ran close to the door and stepped outside briefly. Dickson followed him, but by the time Dickson had got to the bottom of the steps, Potter had slipped to his left and re-entered the building. With obvious delight, Potter locked the door. The rest of the class emitted a cheer and continued with their vegetable chorus.

Potter was suspended for a week, Dickson was pensioned off at the end of term and the rest of the class had Saturday morning detention for a month. Ed often invoked this story whenever he wanted to talk about the intoxicating feeling of revolution. The mass of his woodwork class, worm down by the sterile conformity of existence, had risen up and caused havoc. For one moment in their dull, otherwise meaningless, conveyor-belt lives they had real power. The birds had been roused by the one.

'I'm sorry I walked out of the café the other day. I can be a bit impulsive at times, you know. I just… I was just in a bad mood. You know it can happen. You know.' He seems genuinely apologetic and yet something stills nags.

'I might have a chance to work in Vienna next year.'

My comment is a lie, not even an exaggeration, but I want to direct the conversation.

'Great!'

Ed feigns interest.

'Just think, afternoons having *Kaffee und Kuchen!* You can come and visit me!'

Ed nods, picks up his glass and drinks. He wants to move off the subject, he feels uncomfortable.

'Course nothing beats beer!'

Ed smiles, red returns to his cheeks. I don't want to upset my best friend tonight.

S EVEN THIRTY. I jump out of bed. I'm so excited and I just can't hide it! I point myself in the right direction: the bathroom. I sing merrily in the shower, I munch away happily at the breakfast table.

'God! I hope you're not going to be so bloody happy every day you go to work.'

Emma, one of my housemates, sighs and opens her cupboard. For some reason she decided to choose one of the bottom cupboards when we were sharing out kitchen space. She leans over and sticks her head into the blackhole. A few moments later she reappears clutching a packet of cornflakes.

'Got any milk?' she says, sounding hopeful as she peers into the fridge light.

'Um. No, sorry.'

'Oh,' she sighs, 's'pose I'll have to make do with black coffee.' She clasps her mug with both hands, pointing the handle straight at my heart, and says, 'Tom, I met this bloke last night.' Off she goes again. She is the luckiest girl alive.

*

I read the *Guardian* with a broad smile on my face, the other commuters just scowl. My jolly disposition is deadened slightly as I cross Southwark Bridge. As I approach the building, I take two deep breaths and enter.

New jobs are daunting, especially when they are your first. I've washed windows, pulled pints, cleaned floors, but this is my first *real* job. I am shown the coffee machine, the toilets and am forced to shake hands with everyone. Names, names, hundreds of different names, hundreds of different faces. It's easy for them, they just have one name to remember, an insignificant name at that. I, on the other hand, have to remember the names of all the sub-editors, secretaries and even the guy in the post room. Fortunately, I do not have to take a test.

My boss Charles – he prefers to call himself a mentor – has asked me to begin by doing some background research, I have until the end of the day to come up with some ideas for his next article. Books to my left, magazines to my right and a desk with a PC and a telephone. Welcome to the wonderful world of work!

'Hi! Or should I say *dobry denny!*' he laughed. Is this person trying to speak Russian to me? 'I'm Tony!'

A hand is thrust into my face. I shake it.

'I play squash. Do you play squash? I play every day. We should play together sometime!'

I nod. 'I', he pauses and looks around him, 'cover foreign affairs. And you?'

He is desperate to impress. Red socks, flowery tie and a smarmy smile. I take an instant dislike to this git. Should I make a joke? Probably not a good idea on my first day. Would he understand it? Is this a test? He probably doesn't want to listen to the sound of my voice when he could be speaking.

'I'm just a lowly graduate trainee.' I emit the line matter-of-factly, turn toward my desk and proceed with my research. I can see him scampering off into the distance; he obviously thought that my desk, so close to the distinguished columnist, Charles Madrid, indicated superiority.

Laughter can be heard to my left and right. Bill, one of my colleagues whose name I can remember, comes over and slaps me on the back.

'Glad to see you know how to deal with prats like Tony!' He adds, 'I'm sorry, but Tony is such a sad networker he will introduce himself to a coffee machine if he thinks he can get something out of it. We, and I apologise for this, told him a distinguished journalist from Moscow was joining today.'

'I hope all my colleagues won't be that bad!' I add with a sly grin on my face.

'They aren't! The talentless ones tend to be the worst. They know their only chance of advancement is to be friends with everyone who's somebody.'

'And are *you* somebody?' I ask, a devious smile emblazoned across my visage.

'Oh no!' he replies in comic vein.

'Well, I better not talk to you then! I'm a busy man!'

With that I turn around, but instantly turn back laughing. I'm off to a flyer!

★

Charles has asked to see me at five. I have worked methodically through a number of publications. A few ideas have been scribbled in my notebook. It is now four fifty. I have ten minutes to prepare myself. I want to perform well today. Whatever people say about clichés, they do contain grains of truth. First impressions count.

I cast my eye over my ideas. All my ideas refer to Germany, Russia or Britain. I've shown no initiative, no novelty, nothing outside my chosen specialist subjects. Even the topics I've chosen do not seem to be covering new ground. A wave of disappointment washes over my soul. I look desperately through the articles to my left. Surely I can find something else. No! No! Five o'clock.

I rise from my chair and walk over to Charles's door. 'Got to be confident, Tom!' I keep telling myself.' I throw in a palliative: his expectations are bound to be low on the first day. I raise my head and knock. I follow the command to enter. Charles is sitting at his desk frantically writing. His eye skips to the clock as I take a step into his office. He has a pile of papers on his desk, but they are obscured by a line of photograph frames. He stops his frantic typing for a second.

'Look, Tom, sorry to be a pain on your first day, but I've gotta get this piece done. They want three five, not five six. I'm gonna be tied up. Why don't you go home and we'll talk about it at nine tomorrow? Sorry!'

The wave has dumped me on a beach, a haven for a night. I have time to build a shelter.

I T'S SATURDAY NIGHT in the big smoke. The pubs have just closed, spilling their customers on to the pavement. Four lads are attempting to sing a song about swinging chariots. Their voices are not in unison, not even in tune. One seems to have forgotten the words, he is just 'lalaing' his way through the chorus. To their right, a short girl with black shoulder-length hair has her arms around a stocky man with fiery red hair. She gazes into his eyes, closes her eyelids slowly and pushes her mouth towards his. He crooks his neck a little more. Facial unity has been achieved.

Susi's mouth is wide open; a silent scream emanates, while she moves her clenched fists from side to side in rapid succession. She wants to go dancing. She begins to circle the tired and the drunk. We do not have any energy. Sarah can only stay upright thanks to Derek's solid frame. I am just shattered. A week of work is too much for an old man like me. Susi has been lying in bed all week, relaxing, eating, watching daytime TV. I, on the other hand, have been slaving away producing suggestion after suggestion for my distinguished boss Charles. Sometimes even a hefty pay packet is not adequate compensation for the loss of freedom.

Ed's battered copy of *A Theory of Justice* is clearly visible, poking its head above his pocket. The others in the group of ten are behind a veil of ignorance. Should they risk it all and go dancing with Susi? They do not know the type of club she will take them to. Wild, bohemian, perverted, straight, mixed, Eighties, techno, retro; all are within easy reach. The dens of iniquity draw in those who wander too close to the magnet.

Ed seems distant. He is walking apart from the group, lost in his own train of thought. Hands are firmly ensconced in pockets, eyes glued to the road. His gaze is not distracted by the enticing lure of Chinese food. The aroma is captivating. My mouth begins to salivate. The thought of duck with green peppers in black bean sauce rolls around in my mind. My taste buds want cuisine to roll around with them.

We turn the corner on to Gerrard Street, Chinese restaurants to the left, Chinese restaurants to the right. I walk forward, but move to the side. I am drawn to a menu advertising cheap food. My eye, aided by the tip of my right hand, runs down the menu. There, at number thirty-eight, is my nirvana. I repeat it to myself, 'Duck with Green Peppers in Black Bean Sauce', first slowly and then curtly, A hand drags me away. The hand is feminine, the skin soft, the owner is Susi, but it is pulling me away from my desires. I don't want women, just a happy stomach.

'Never mind, Tommy Wommy, maybe next week! We're going dancing!'

I wince.

We find – correction – Susi finds a club. All the men seem to be ten foot tall with wall-to-wall muscles and all the women straight from the catwalks of Milan. Half of our group have made their excuses and left; the remainder are sitting at a table enjoying the brief calm before the storm. Susi is as vibrant as her red dress. Her face, not usually plastered with lipstick, has two lines of the richest red, bold and distinctive.

'Aaahhh!' Susi yells and jumps up suddenly, her arm raised towards the ceiling, a look of pure ecstasy on her face. 'Come on!' she implores the rest of us huddled around our drinks, 'It's the Bee Gees! Let's boogie!'

We rise at varying speeds. I have forgotten about number thirty-eight and jump up, Ed sighs, throws his head back, stretches out his arms and forces his legs to take the strain. Sarah, however, remains seated, her head is happily resting on her arm, her arm on the wooden table.

The dance floor is full of hot sweaty bodies. There is the usual collection of introverted and extroverted dancers. The former remain stationary, move their shoulders forward and back in time with the Music. The latter do everything else. An extrovert is dancing away to my left; she is wearing a black dress with pieces of red and orange material sewn on. Her hair is being thrown from side to side. Her figure stands out as a magnet for those who care to look. I turn towards her and begin to snap out of introverted mood. She moves left, I mirror her action. She moves to the right, I follow. She turns, I follow. She looks up, in anticipation of a particular face. Mine does not fit. She turns ninety degrees and engages a man to my right. Good movement, but just can't capitalise on the scoring chances I create. Wasn't that what my old football coach said?

Ed is following the greatest extrovert of the lot, Susi. She glides around the dance floor effortlessly. Somehow, people move out of the way allowing her to pass. As soon as Ed arrives the gatekeeper closes the route. He has to navigate an alternative route. Susi is distant, always over there. Always setting off on her own paths without telling her fellow travellers where she is going.

*

We went up on to the dance floor for one dance, but we stayed for an hour. Ed and I have left Susi dancing. Her energy seems to know no bounds. Sweat is pouring, legs are aching, mouths are parched. I volunteer to purchase some refreshment. The bar is busy. I use the whole range of hand signals to indicate to anyone who stands in my way I want to get to the bar. Most oblige. Others stand there rooted to their spot. They are tough characters in leather jackets. They want to impress their 'bit of skirt'. They are not pushovers.

I have to order three times. The music is so loud, the barmaid cannot hear. Am I getting old? Music, it's just too loud these days. In my day... Tom, you're only twenty-two years old. The prime of your life is still out there in front of you. I buy bottles, not just because pints are so expensive, but bottles are easier to carry. I will not run the risk of spilling a pint and upsetting a lunatic.

'How's it goin' with Susi? Good?'

'Fine. Although she seems to have a voracious appetite...' The last part of the sentence is lost in the din.

'What?' I ask, my face screwed up, desperate to hear the answer.

'Fine, really well, thanks,' Ed replies, a small nod suggesting that both mouth and chin agree with the statement. 'But', he adds after a short pause, 'she's such a free spirit... I don't think she's a... God, I hate to use the word it sounds so afternoon chat show, a *relationship* person.'

The truth has been promulgated. I can just nod.

'What's the talent like at work?' asks Ed, pushing his head forward in order to hear the answer.

'You know me,' I say, putting on my best wanky accent, 'I don't like to mix business and pleasure.'

'You mean there are sexy women, but they're not interested in you.'

I smile and nod. There is no riposte to the truth. If only Radka were here.

S HE IS MOVING towards me, her naked body dancing in the moonlight. I move closer to her, she greets me and begins to prod my arm.

The bus has stopped. The driver is standing over me, looking at me and prodding me with his left hand. 'Hello! Hello! Warsaw! Warsaw!' I am baffled. Does he think I am a clandestine wartime radio or something? 'Warsaw!' he repeats, pointing out of the window. I peer through the pane of glass. It looks like a bus station, but is this really Warsaw? There are only three or four other buses in the station. Surely this can't be the capital of Poland? Warsaw is the terminus, so why are there people still on the bus?

'This Warsaw? Centre?' My words are slow and pointed. They provoke a reaction of nods from both the driver and the old woman sitting to my right. Who am I to argue? I've never before been to this city in the heart of Europe.

I turn round. Mick and Clara are in each other's arms, Ed is staring straight ahead. 'This is Warsaw, Ed!'

'It doesn't look like bloody Warsaw to me!'

'Look, the driver has assured me. This is Warsaw!'

Ed is not convinced. He looks tired and unhappy; he always sleeps badly on buses. It makes him cantankerous.

'I'm not moving. If this is Warsaw why the hell are there still loads of people on the bus?' he asks. He crosses his arms and sits tight. He ain't prepared to budge an inch.

I can feel the driver behind me. He wants to move off; he cannot understand why these foreigners won't get off his bus. Mick and Clara have returned from their all too brief sojourn in the land of nod. The old lady in front is nodding, pointing out of the window and saying, 'Warsaw! Warsaw!'

I pick up my rucksack and place in on my backside. Mick and Clara slowly follow suit.

'Come on! Ed, this is Warsaw! Come on!'

'Don't you fucking start. I'm not getting off this fucking bus! This is not fucking Warsaw!' Ed's eyes are bloodshot just like his mood. He puts his hands behind his head and stares at me. 'I'm staying here!' he says.

'Come on, Ed!' chips in Clara. 'This is Warsaw!'

Ed is not persuaded by feminine charm.

'I'm not getting off this fucking bus!'

The vulgar vocabulary is understood by all those within earshot. It is the one disadvantage of having one's mother tongue as the world language. The driver wanders back up the aisle. He repeats his little mantra about the capital of Poland, the old lady joins in the chorus. Mick and Clara sling their rucksacks over their shoulders and begin to wander towards the door. I give Ed one more look. He is determined to sit in his seat; he is not prepared to move. I smile at the driver, who seems relieved we've finally understood that we are in Warsaw.

As the three of us walk towards the main building, I look back and see Ed. I beckon him over with my hand. He rises from his seat and storms off the bus. He runs to catch up with us, an annoyed look on his face. When he reaches the grey building, he throws his rucksack down and adds, 'You can fucking sort this out!'

Mick and Clara seem shocked by Ed's outburst. He can be irritating sometimes, caught up in his latest philosopher, or winning an argument. Ed hates losing arguments, but he usually wins and is at least outwardly gracious when he does end up on the losing side. Why is he being so cantankerous? He looks ill, perhaps he is just in desperate need of some sleep. My nerves are always a little frayed whenever I've missed out on my regular eight hours snoozing.

I wander around the building. Polish looks incomprehensible. Clusters of consonants, lines through 'l's, long words. The citizens of the capital are busy going about their morning business. It may only be five thirty in the morning, but already bread is being bought and men in black suits are walking purposefully. A middle-aged woman with a copy of what looks like a heavyweight paper is walking in my direction. Pangs of doubt about language trouble me. German would probably be unwise, Russian equally unsuitable. The legacy of history leaves such an awful taste in one's mouth at times. I decide to revert to my mother tongue.

'Excuse me,' I step forward and pose the question, 'do you know how to get into the centre of Warsaw, please?'

A frown grows on the lady's face. Her head shifts to one side; she points to her ear. I repeat, this time stressing the words Warsaw, centre and please. She raises her finger and the frown is gone.

'*Tramvaj shest*,' she says, holding up six fingers. Her finger points outside. '*Shest, seeks*,' she says.

'Tickets? *Billeti?*' I ask.

She laughs, shakes her head and points at her watch. It's too early. Don't worry about it. I thank her and make my way back to my fellow travellers.

'Tram number six! Come on!'

My enthusiasm doesn't transmit itself to Mick, Ed or Clara. They are lying there spreadeagled, enjoying the early-morning Warsaw sunshine. I repeat myself. Nothing stirs, nobody seems the least bit interested in listening to the messenger.

'I know the way to the centre! Come with me!'

The others do not seem captivated. They have endured a long and enervating journey. They are tired and hungry. They want to be in the centre. They want to indulge themselves in the activities of the centre. Mick can have a McDonald's, Clara can buy some smelly soap, and Ed can drink and pontificate in welcoming bars. Only I, however, want to move.

I pick up my rucksack and stride purposefully towards the tram stop. The others begin to move. Ed is the first to catch up.

'Why can't we take it a little slower? Wait here just a little longer? It's not even six o'clock yet! What's the rush? Please, mate.'

'Look! Let's get into the centre. We can eat and rest there! Come on!'

Ed doesn't seem that enthralled. He wants to eat, relax and take his time.

'You know we have to follow you. You are the guide! You speak all the languages. Without you we'd be totally lost!' His outburst is over, but he adds, 'Have you bought any tickets?'

I shake my head.

'What if we get caught?'

'We won't. It's too early. Nobody will be checking at this time.'

Right on cue, a tram trundles up to the stop. The doors fling open. We board and sit on the red plastic chairs, our rucksacks perched on top of our laps. The outskirts of Warsaw hurtle past the tram, while we are thrown from side to side as the tram negotiates the bends.

The tram judders to a halt. Four men wearing bomber jackets and jeans board. The tram is virtually empty and yet they linger by the doors. They look up and down the carriage, but still they do not sit themselves down on the comfortable red plastic chairs. They look suspicious. A cabal mulling over its next act. I feel uncomfortable. They are stocky men. We are – with the exception of Mick – weak and feeble. Neither Ed nor Mick seem to take any notice of these men.

A word is spoken, something is thrust into my face. They are not violent criminals. They are ticket inspectors. I feign incomprehension. I look up at the leader of the gang, my best innocent look on my face. The fair-haired inspector just stares back at me, his blue eyes piercing my guilty soul.

'English,' I say.

'Do you have ticket?' he responds. I shake my head; it droops in shame. I feel embarrassed.

'Sorry, you must pay!'

There is no venom in his voice. I begin to berate myself. Why didn't I go out of my way to find where the tickets are sold. You are a daft cunt, Tom. The 'C-word' is the strongest in the English language. It upsets women. It is horrible. Today, however, Mr Thomas Reed, you deserve to be described as the lowest of the low. Not only could you not be bothered to find out where the tickets were sold, you've also dragged your friends into the ignominy.

I look up at the piercing blue eyes.

'How much?'

He takes out his sheet and points at a figure. I employ a little mental arithmetic. Twenty-five dollars each, that's two days' budget each. I know I do not have that amount of *zloty*.

'I have only dollars and *Deutschmark*. I came from Lithuania.'

The inspector doesn't seem to be buying my story.

'Can I pay in *Deutschmark?*'

The inspector moves his head quickly from side to side.

'You come with me to exchange,' says the ticket official firmly but without malice.

I nod. Mick looks at me venomously. He thought I had all the answers. He thought I knew everything. He put his trust in me and I have shattered all his illusions.

★

'I'm sorry, guys. I didn't realise we'd get caught.'

'You were in such a hurry to reach the centre. Couldn't we have waited just a little longer?'

Ed looks at me across the café table. His finger is waving. He is annoyed.

'I would have been happier to have waited on the outskirts for a little longer and had more time to enjoy the fact we'd arrived in Warsaw.' He pauses momentarily and then adds, 'I mean what are we doing now. Sitting around, drinking coffee. Come on! We could've done that back there. Sometimes', he leans over the table and lowers his voice, his finger pointing straight at the bridge of my nose, 'you are a bloody know-it-all.'

I feel guilty. I am guilty, but I have to respond. I have to at least plead something in mitigation.

'Well, we're here now in the centre of Warsaw, enjoying a really', I glance around me, 'good American beefburger. Look,' I say, pointing at Mick sitting at an adjacent table, 'Mick's enjoying his burger.'

'Twenty-five dollars for a short tram journey. The bus from Lithuania only cost us the equivalent of about five dollars.'

'I can't fucking afford it,' chimes in Mick.

I decide not to continue the argument. I've lost. I should let it go.

★

Charles Madrid, distinguished columnist and my boss, is a very busy man. No sooner have we started to speak about interesting stories I've found from hours delving through the media's gargantuan output, than the phone rings again. Another phone call, another language. He is speaking Italian. It is fluent and, at least to a layman like me, spoken with a wonderful accent.

What does one do in such a circumstance? To gaze around the room is easy, but it looks as if I am just wasting time waiting for him to finish speaking. My eye cannot help drifting. A tall bookshelf stands to his right. It is crammed with dictionaries of every conceivable language. Can he really speak all these languages or is he just showing off? On the wall there are photos of Charles receiving awards. Judging by the size of the bow ties and the length of his hair they were taken many years ago. In one photo he is perched on his knees, a flak jacket covering his chest, the boots of soldiers to his left and right. How heroic! Charles places his hand over the receiver and looks in my direction.

'Sorry, Tom. I think this is going to be a long call. Please carry on with the Chubais thing. Cheers.'

With that order, I rise from the chair and glance again at those dictionaries and photos, knowledge, talent and achievement stare back at me. Although Charles is a warm and friendly man, it is all rather too intimidating. I still have got to travel a long way down the long and winding road.

I LOOK AT MY alarm clock. It's seven thirty on a Saturday, time to rise. Time to jump out of bed and get ready. Time to don my best shirt and tie. I look at my alarm clock again. If only I could stop time. If only I could stop it, just for twenty minutes. Last night was supposed to be a light evening, just a quiet beer after work. Charles, however, had been really pleased with his piece on contemporary Russian politics. I was considered to have contributed to his success, so he'd taken me out for a celebratory drink.

I had explained to him my old university mate, Alan, was getting married the next day, but he just kept saying, 'Just one more then.' I glance over towards my suit. A few grains of rice have somehow managed to lodge themselves in my lapel. Slowly, teasingly, my memory begins to feed me with more facts about last night, curry, beer, taxi home. My mind is sharpened by these thoughts. I didn't take a taxi home last night. How had I got home? Disturbing images begin to float around in my head. My God how *did* I get home? My, my, my bowels are moving. At least it gets me out of bed.

I am disgusted by the state of the toilet. I feel ashamed. In one of Susi's favourite expressions, I must have been 'talking to God on the big white telephone'. The expression engenders a smile, followed by a sharp pain in my abdomen. What will the others in the house say? My stomach is obviously unhappy with what my mouth fed it last night. I shiver. I pick up the toilet roll and wipe the worst excesses off the seat cover. I look at myself in the shaving mirror; my eyes are bloodshot, my face a white sheet.

I sit on the toilet and stare at the opposite wall. The pastel shade of blue is however too much. It is too garish. I place my head in my hands and hope the morning will start again. I can hear a thudding. The noise grates. My ear-drums hurt.

'Is anyone in there? Can you hurry up?'

It is housemate Emma.

Her beautiful, melodic voice is lost on me, on this of all mornings. Why can't she just go away? Go away, Emma, please! I want to wrap myself up in a blanket and hide. Hide from this world, hide from this cruel and vindictive morning.

'Tom! It's you, isn't it! Come on, hurry up! I've got to be at work by eight thirty. When's your train? Shouldn't you have left by now?'

The truth hurts. The truth cannot be ignored. The truth won't go away.

'Sorry, Emma,' I pause for breath, 'I...' I need another gulp of oxygen. 'I... need to take a shower.'

'Look, Tom, I've seen you before in your pants. Can I just come in and use the washbasin?'

It is a perfectly reasonable request. On a normal morn-ing, when I wasn't just recovering from a heavy drinking session, I would assent immediately, but I can see remnants of the curry which need to be cleared away. I plead for two seconds. I race. I mop up all the morsels quickly, but carefully. Sometimes an order from a woman can be a good thing. I open the door. Emma is standing there, tall, elegant and top of the morning.

'You look good,' she declares as she brushes past me.

'Do I?' I say, completely nonplussed by the comment. How can she say such a thing now? White face, bloodshot eyes and a look of agony planted on my face. She leans over the washbasin to gain a closer look at her facial features. Her pert breasts are radiating their majesty back towards themselves. I gulp. I am feeling aroused, Suddenly I realise something dreadful, something beyond awful, worse than terrible. This is hell. I'm wearing boxer shorts. The thought entertains my mind. My arousal increases. This is my housemate! She's got a lover, who's a good mate of mine! Why am I aroused? I was drunk last night. I should have fisherman's limp or something. What do I do? Slowly sneak out? Yes! Yes! Turn and walk away.

'Where are you going? Are you embarrassed about your erection, or something?'

Her voice is loud and matter-of-fact. The words echo around my empty head. She seems to display no sense of tact, she didn't even employ a euphemism.

'Tom! Stop turning round! You were completely pissed last night and should', she says, stopping momentarily to apply her lipstick to her moist lips, backwards and forwards across her succulent lips, 'be limp, but you are aroused by me. I take that', she continues while brushing her hair, 'as a compliment.' She turns towards me and says, 'I never thought I looked so sexy at this time of the morning.'

With that passing comment she blows me a kiss and strides purposefully out of the door. The whirlwind has gone. My defences were too weak, the structural engineer had done a poor job. Now begins the task of repairing the damage. Before I have time to begin the job of reparations, Emma pokes her head around the door.

'By the way, both your dad and your sister rang last night. They both want you to call back today.'

I stay in the bathroom for another twenty minutes. I feel I need a shower to cleanse my body and soul of last night and this morning. Emma. Emma is a wonderful housemate. She is funny, tolerant, pays her bills on time and doesn't play Metallica at full volume at three in the morning, but she does love to gossip. Our little encounter will entertain all those who work on her magazine. 'Fuck!' I ejaculate the word. Yes, I know it's the wrong word. I know it harbours certain connotations, has certain meanings in common parlance, but in my own bathroom, my own little sanctuary – it's the little boys' room after all – I should be able to say what I want! Besides, I've totally embarrassed myself already today. Vomit, badly timed erections, please cover me up, please hide me.

*

I arrive late at the train station. My stomach is still churning. My head is still throbbing. I wonder momentarily whether I should proceed or whether I should wave the white flag and concede victory to the god of retribution.

Paddington station is full of people either rushing around in top gear or standing and gazing transfixed by the timetable. Few seem just to wander slowly and carefully. The exception is the litter man, a modern-day superhero. He glides towards me gracefully. The green bin is loaded on to his trolley. He pushes the green monster towards his find, a pile of hamburger wrappers and empty soft drink cans. Slowly he bends down, gathers them up and throws them into the green machine. They have lost their freedom. They will never be allowed to blow around Paddington station again.

The spell of the timetable has gone. To my left and to my right people are moving, bags are being slung on shoulders, children are being told, 'Platform four'. I gaze up at the repository of all knowledge. Through a series of dots cleverly arranged, I see the Bath train is ready to swim.

AFTER OUR LITTLE tiff, our small difference of opinion, we decide to have a morning to ourselves. Mick and Clara want to eat McDonald's all day, I want to see the Chopin museum and Ed wants to rest his weary head. He is complaining of chest pains, his skin looks blotchy, his throat has a large unmalleable frog lodged in its core. I feel guilty, I feel at least partially responsible for his state of health. He is perfectly civil to me, imploring me to go out and enjoy the delights of Warsaw, to visit the Chopin museum, have a beer, relax. He just wants to lie there, read his books and drink coffees and teas.

The others refuse my offers to pay their fines. They keep stressing to me that we are a group. All for one and all that stuff from Dumas. I feel guilty. I forced them to go to the centre, to the bright lights before they wanted to. I cost them twenty-five dollars each. I resolve to buy them at least a little present, a small palliative for their suffering.

The centre of Warsaw is picturesque. A vibrant sea of colours radiate themselves to all who dare to peek. They aren't the original buildings, but then those benign uncles, Joe and Adolf, weren't too keen on the original inhabitants.

A beautiful woman with legs the length of the Danube walks up to me. I know Warsaw isn't on the Danube, but these legs are long. Her rich dark eyes penetrate my soul; her perfect figure entertains my mind and body. She is wearing a short white skirt that displays supremely her lower limbs. A white sash draped across her body only highlights her curves. She thrusts something towards me. This perfect specimen of womanhood is giving me something. I don't want to take my eyes off her high cheekbones. She motions downwards with her eyes. Everything she does is sexy. There in her hand is a thin white stick with an orange section tagged on the end. She is trying to encourage me to smoke. A beautiful woman, who would make a fine Mrs Reed, is utilising her talents to encourage others to smoke. Priorities, priorities. Where are they? I take the cigarette, but keep looking at her and smiling. She sees I have succumbed to her charm. She smiles and turns her head. I am only interesting as a business transaction. How gratifying!

*

My guidebook tells me this is the place. There does not seem to be any movement. Surely, the place should be buzzing. This is Chopin's house. The greatest composer Poland has produced. Beethoven might have written a few decent symphonies, Mozart a couple of good piano concertos and a few operas, but Chopin wrote all those beautiful, melodic, romantic, captivating pieces for piano. He showed you only needed one instrument, one collection of black and white keys, to create masterpieces. The tourists and citizens of Warsaw obviously don't agree. Come to think of it, Mum always thought Chopin was third-rate. But Mum thought Gilbert and Sullivan were good, so her opinions count for bollocks.

I open the door slowly. I am convinced the museum must be shut today, it would explain the dearth of visitors. Inside the entrance hall are three old ladies sipping coffee and munching cakes. No sign of any other visitors. The ladies stop their conversation in mid-flow as I enter. One rises from her chair and smiles at me. I reciprocate and nod my head. I reach in my pocket and find my international student card and a large banknote. She smiles and says some amount, at least I assume it must be an amount, because the sentence ends with a word that resembles '*zloty*'.

As I pick up my change, which consists of thousands and thousands of *zloty* notes, I proceed towards the first room. One of the other old ladies scuttles past me. A moment ago she was sitting so serenely drinking coffee, why is she running? Was it something I did? She rushes into the first room, switches on the light and, because this is the Chopin Museum after all, she switches on some soft tranquil music. They are switching on the lights and the music just for me! I feel honoured.

The old lady tries her very best to be discreet, but she cannot hide the fact that I am the only visitor in the museum. She smiles at me as I enter every room, the music and lights having just been turned on. Ten out of ten for energy efficiency. Her routine is to wait about five minutes after I have entered the room, then walk back with a slip of paper in her hand, or a potted plant, or on one occasion a musical instrument which resembled a flute and look to see how far round the room I have got. In one room, unconsciously, I linger and linger. I am fascinated by Chopin's piano. I want to reach out and touch it, but I know I shouldn't. The old lady walks in, this time with a small duster, lightly touching various pictures with her cleaning contraption. She is disconcerted. I can feel her nervous movement. She begins to straighten some pictures, casting sideways glances at me after every picture has been altered.

She moves over towards me and begins to talk. Her Polish is fast, furious and utterly baffling. I can understand nothing apart from the word Chopin. She stops in mid-flow, as if someone has just hit the pause button. She looks up at me, her dark brown eyes desperately trying to fathom out what is this creature that stands before her.

'*Deutsch? Kommen Sie aus Deutschland?*'

I move my head rapidly from left to right, but respond to her in German, informing her of my origins.

'English!' she declares loudly in my vernacular. 'I love the English language! I love England and America!'

To accompany this declaration of love for my language and country, she raises both her thumbs and smiles. This act, which I always associate with a friend known affectionately as Smeggy, I find disconcerting. This old lady is impeccably dressed, a single thread of pearls adorns her neck, a flowery brooch enlivens an otherwise rather plain blouse. She is the diametrical opposite of Smeggy.

She begins to recount to me the personal history of the great composer. She dwells on his lovers and drags me over to the side of the room to observe a love letter written when the young composer was, as she put it, 'about your age'. What does that mean? Is she saying I should have a girlfriend? How does she know? Is she trying it on with me? Get real, Tom! She's just attempting to enable me to empathise with the life of this composer who died years ago. She wants to bring his story to life.

After a long conversation with her, I leave the room and the museum. As the door closes, I wonder whether anybody else will open the wooden door today and set foot into the wonderful world of Chopin. The *Funeral March* begins to reverberate around my mind. How apt.

Part Five

Till Death Us Do Part

I ARRIVE AT the wedding late according to my scrupulously arranged timetable, but early enough to save face. Alan's fiancée, Melanie, has yet to display her white dress to her intended. Everyone else, however, is there sitting, kneeling, praying, glancing, spying, resting, twiddling thumbs. Alan is standing by the altar, his brother Michael to his left, his family and friends behind them. I am welcomed by somebody, given an order of service and told to sit in the centre somewhere on the left. Who tipped them off that I am a *Guardian* reader?

I see Robert Smythe to my left, fiddling with his buttonhole. Nobody is sitting next to him. He looks conspicuously single. If only all those women sitting on the other side of the church, across the great divide, knew what riches he had they would be flocking. Robert doesn't advertise his wealth, he spends it discreetly. His fingers have been singed in the past by fire-breathing women desperate to burn his money. In consequence, he has modified his accent. No longer is it pure Etonian English, now his vowels are tinged with South London. Peckham meets Oxford. Rodney Trotter meets Hugh Grant. As I sit down, he whispers a little, "'Ello.' I reciprocate. Two honorary South Londoners sharing a little greeting. Lovely!

I straighten my jacket, feel my collar and glance briefly at the order of service. Five hymns, a sermon and communion. I cannot concentrate on the beautifully embossed paper. Someone has, no doubt, spent hours burning the midnight oil to create such exquisite paper. My eye wanders. Hats. All I can see is a sea of hats, blues, greys, reds, whites. All have such large brims to shelter the delicate faces. A large man is trying his very best to discreetly run around the church for some reason or other, but he only succeeds in attracting everyone's attention. His tiptoeing attracts glares like farting in an enclosed place.

Hello! Hello! Hello! Oh, my God! Over there! Look! No, don't look! She's looking. My mind is racing, my jaw dropping, my heart pounding. Long brown hair, emerald eyes, long legs, figure-hugging clothes, I try not to look. I am still wearing my boxer shorts. She appears to be sitting alone. I could be there. If I hadn't sat next to Rob, I could have placed my posterior to the left of this beauty. Her long white gloves snake up her arm towards her ocean-blue dress. I want to swim and drown. If I can't swim, I want to paddle. If I can't paddle, I want to dip my toe. If I can't dip my toe, I want at least to walk along the beach.

Throughout the singing, the exchanging of vows, the long ponderous sermon, I cannot think of anything other than the foxy lady on the right of the church. The priest, a large avuncular man, with a broad grin permanently on his face, tries hard to deflect my attention. He fails. I know he probably wants to save my life and give me eternal life in the land flowing with milk and honey, but I want short-term hedonism, I don't want to impose limitations upon myself, I just want to satisfy my lust. He talks of the beautiful couple, their love, their place with God. I cannot think of others, just her and me.

Bells ring out. They proclaim the joyous marriage of the happy couple, Alan and Melanie, hoorah! Hoorah! The newly-weds walk hand in hand out of the church. Happiness radiates everywhere. Even the sun decides to join the fray, beaming its benign rays on the deserving couple. My mind is still otherwise occupied. The object of my attention is standing there alone. Has no one else seen her? I shake hands with the bride and bridegroom's parents, and mutter something about the lovely service and the ideal setting. It *is* an ideal setting. A thirteenth-century church nestled in the heart of the Wiltshire countryside, rolling green fields to the left and right. 'Congratulations!' Just one word, but then brevity is the source of wit. Besides, Alan and Mel have had to endure so many people giving them long spiels about the service and the weather and the setting. 'Mel. Sorry to ask such a question on a day like this.' I pause. Should I indicate to her my interest in the long gloves and blue dress, or should I, should I... tact.

'You're wondering who the girl with the blue dress is, aren't you?'

How did she know that? Is she a mind-reader? I nod and look at her enquiringly. Mel seems tickled by the question. It is probably the most original question or comment she's heard today. She leans towards me, licks her lips and says quietly, but with emphasis on every word, 'Why don't you ask Ed?'

I rock back on my heels. 'Ed? What do you mean?' I exclaim rather too loudly. The rest of the accumulated guests look at me disdainfully. 'Where is he?'

Mel stretches out her right arm, pastel-pink nail varnish pointing the way. I follow the bride's finger and decide to follow her instructions. Ed, who was engaged as an usher during the ceremony, looks radiant.

'Hey, Tom! How's it going, my man?' He pronounces the last two words in a broad American accent. He spins around, displaying his top hat and tails to all that care to look. Cole Porter lyrics trip off his tongue and into the public domain.

'Who's the girl in the blue dress? Mel says you know her.'

'It's Natasha.'

I shrug my shoulder to indicate incomprehension. He has answered my question according to strict definition of the words, but my mind is no nearer to understanding why this creature, who oozes sexuality from every pore, is here now? I rotate my right hand to indicate I expect more of an answer Ed repeats the name, as if repetition will yield comprehension, 'Natasha, Natasha. Don't you remember me talking about her?' he asks, a frown beginning to appear on his face.

I'm still nonplussed. 'Doctor Natasha.' He stresses the word doctor. Why? 'God your memory is terrible! Don't you remember?' I shake my head. 'In Warsaw?'

E D LOOKS HAPPY, very happy. It cannot be in consequence of the gift I bought him. A beer glass with an unpronounceable name embossed on the side is a gift, he knows I know, will be one he will appreciate. For once I have been thinking about what others want, not just satisfying my desires or trying to educate.

'Thanks!'

He grabs the beer glass, briefly glances at the design and keeps smiling.

'I had a great day!' he exclaims, jumping up from the chair.

In response to his sudden burst of kinetic energy, I feel forced to sit down. Ed wants to perform. He wants me to watch.

'I went to the Warsaw Hospital for Infectious Diseases!'

He seems like a small child, desperate to tell his work-weary father how he has whittled away another day. I frown, take a sip of water from the large bottle of fizzy French water, and look back at Ed.

'I'm in love!'

The room is silent. The seconds tick away, still silence rules. Ed is captivated by the image of his love. I am perplexed. This morning Ed was tired, ill and cantankerous; this afternoon he is joyous, almost too enthusiastic, too happy. How can anyone's mood swing so violently? I remember once reading, in one of those long, ponderous articles that tend to fill up Sunday supplements, about people who were bitten by a mosquito or something and suffered from delusions and wild mood swings. They were unable to focus on reality. Their minds were captivated by internally produced images swirling around in their minds. Ed does seem distant. He doesn't seem to be focusing on me, or on Clara or Mick!

He has started to skip around the room, shouting out the name 'Natasha', followed by a 'I love you!' or two. Should I humour him? Play along with the game? Or just sit here with a fixed smile nailed on to my face? My God – he hasn't tried to take heroin or LSD, has he? He often speaks about trying various substances to gain affinity with Foucault, John Lennon and Aldous Huxley. He turns sharply towards me; his skipping has ceased. He asks me in all sobriety, 'Well, aren't you going to ask me what she's like?' He *is* truly captivated by someone. He isn't joking! My God, Ed may actually have fallen in love! I now feel ashamed of my cynicism. I motion with both hands rapidly and energetically for him to continue.

'Settle down, children. Are you sitting comfortably? Then we can begin!'

Perhaps he *is* on drugs.

'You know I was feeling pretty ill this morning. Well, I thought rather than pop paracetamol all day, I would try to sort out what was wrong with me body.'

Ed's penchant for speaking in silly accents was taking over again. Scousers rule, okay! Drugs?

'I thought to meself, I'd go and see what our man in Warsaw had to say. So I boogie on down to the embassy and ask the nice man behind the counter, in a posh English accent, of course, "Terribly sorry to disturb you, old chap, but I seem to have a frightful rash all over my body. Is there anything you chaps can do?"'

Ed clears his throat. As he brings his hand towards his lips, I can see his rash is still there in evidence, still radiating contagion to all who care to look.

'Well,' he continues after clearing his throat a second time, 'he told me there was a hospital in Warsaw with doctors who spoke good English. He kindly called them and made me an appointment for two thirty.'

Ed looks at his audience. Mick seems engrossed in his magazine; Clara is just smiling and I'm perched on the edge of my seat desperate to know the identity of the mysterious Natasha. He continues in his normal voice, 'I find the clinic tucked away in the north side of the city; two different trams and a short walk are needed. I walk in, smile at the receptionist and declare my nationality.'

'In English?' I ask.

'Well, I don't speak Polish, do I?' Ed replies curtly.

It was a stupid thing to say, but I felt I needed to redeem myself and show some enthusiasm by asking at least one question. The best-laid plans of mice and men.

'A large Polish doctor examined me and announced in his strong Slavic accent, "I tink you mosst go here." He turns round scribbles something on his pristine white pad and adds, "I will ring. You be there soon. Okay!"'

Mick looks up at Ed's imitation of a Slavic accent. Ed senses we all just want him to cut the waffle and get to the point, the identity of Natasha.

'Well,' Ed continues, 'the doctor made me an appointment at the Warsaw Hospital for Infectious Diseases. When I got there I thought it was the kind of place to pick up infectious disease, rather than be cured of them!'

I smile at Ed's joke; Clara manages a slight chuckle, but Mick has returned to his magazine.

'Anyway, I'm shown into this room. White, white, white. Why are hospital rooms always white?'

Ed doesn't wait for us to answer. It is obviously rhetorical. 'And in she comes. Tall, elegant, long brown hair, emerald eyes, I was cured! But I'm still going back for a check-up tomorrow!'

'To see the dirt,' says Mick.

We all look at him, inquisitive looks staring at him in unison.

'White walls... in hospitals!' Oh, dove from above, come and save us.

E D HAS BORROWED his dad's car for the day; he offers to drive me to the reception. I agree immediately, not just because I can swap anecdotes and have a laugh with my best friend, but I want a closer look at Natasha, Dr Natasha. I have managed to connect a certain doctor and Warsaw. My brain was just a little slow. In mitigation I must plead the continuing effects of my hangover. Everything still seems to be going a little too fast.

The wedding guests divide themselves up without too much fuss. There is the odd granny and long-lost cousin who are without cars, but everyone has put on their generosity hat and offered to convey these souls from the church to the hotel. Natasha walks over towards Ed's car, her blue hat fluttering in the wind. Stop it, Tom, she's your best friend's… she's my best friend's what? Ed and I are approaching the car; I allow my order of service to fall from my grip. Ed bends down to pick it up. I bend down, put my arm on Ed's back and whisper, 'Ed, can I ask you a personal question?'

We must look terribly conspiratorial.

'Yes.'

'You've come with Natasha to the wedding?' My voice rises on the last word to indicate a question.

'Ten out of ten for observation.'

'Are you? Why with Natasha?'

'The invite said Ed and guest.'

I pause, pat his back and ask, 'Why aren't you here with Susi? Have you finished with her?'

Ed stands up and looks down at me, the rims of his spectacles glinting in the sunlight.

'I came with Natasha, because she is a beautiful woman. I love her, and besides, the winner of the Teflon prize for emotional attachments has decided to leave me on the kitchen floor. I've been there, done that. She wasn't worth all the hassle, all the hours of chase, all the hours of agony. She's a good laugh, but a crap lover and she only cares about one person. *"Le soleil, c'est* Susi"*.* Look, can we just forget her? And don't talk to Natasha about her all right... Please!'

Ed speaks so quickly, the words trip off his tongue, merging into each other. I stand up and look him straight in the face. Anger still burns. Not for me, not for my questioning. He knew someone would ask him today. A whole day at a wedding, when partners, girlfriends, boyfriends are on display, comments are made, leering looks are made, when 'Don't they make a lovely couple' is repeated as a mantra. His anger is directed at the woman who would have been here if things hadn't gone wrong.

'What are you two talking about?'

Rich Slavic vowels fill the car park. Warm Slavic vowels radiate from the beautiful, intelligent woman who is leaning, ever so slightly provocatively, over the car bonnet.

I turn towards Ed, pat him on the shoulder and say quietly, 'You look as if you've found a supersub to fill her shoes in super speedy time!'

A cheeky grin emerges on Ed's face.

'Maybe, she will do a David Fairclough and score late on, giving the team a famous victory!'

Ed looks bemused. He isn't a Liverpool fan, why should he know trivia like that? Ed is, after all, not a trivial man.

ANOTHER CAPITAL CITY, another train station. Why do train stations look the same? Why doesn't some radical architect come up with a novel design? Someone probably has, but it was, no doubt, rejected on cost grounds, or spurious aesthetic grounds.

Mick is sitting absorbed in his magazine. Clara is racing through her thriller; she wants to finish it before we leave. Ed has a broad grin like a Cheshire cat. He met his doctor last night for a drink. He bought the food, she the wine and they supped together from the cup of happiness. The aftertaste still lingers. He doesn't seem depressed that he will never see his white-coated healer again. He seems – although he would berate me for the use of the adjective – very philosophical about it.

'We knew we will probably never set eyes on each other again, so we just decided to enjoy the moment,' he told me earlier on this morning.

How mature! How adult! How can he not hanker? Or is he just hiding it really well? Is this man I see before me made of sterner stuff than I?

The train pulls out of the station slowly, but not smoothly. Ed stands by the window, gulping in the intoxicating air of the Polish capital. Perhaps he is starting to hanker? Yet his expression is still full of joy, full of happiness. Blessed are those who sup from the cup of happiness.

Mick leans over to me and asks, 'Where we heading?'

'Budapest, via Krakow,' I respond, my eyes not shifting from my novel. I sense in Mick's voice a wish the journey was over, or at least nearing its completion. He looks tired. Bags are beginning to appear under his eyes. He is probably craving his own bed, a pint in the Dog and Duck and a portion of fish and chips from Mickie's Fish Bar.

Talk of food stimulates thoughts in my mind. Baked beans. Baked beans, how I love them. The Italians gave us pasta and pizza, the French *haute cuisine*, the Russians caviar. What have the English given the culinary world? Baked beans in tomato sauce, fish and chips, and salt and vinegar crisps. Salt and vinegar crisps and a pint of Guinness. Nirvana. Nirvana.

My musings on the contribution of the green and pleasant land to world cuisine is brought to a halt by a butch ticket collector demanding some evidence of our payment. Mick fishes his ticket out of his pocket and as a reward receives a large hole. I hand over mine and receive the same reward, although this time he offers what sounds like a thank you. Clara has inadvertently placed her ticket in her money-belt. What's the point in having a money-belt, if you have to fumble around whenever an inspector wants to see your ticket? Clara fumbles and fumbles. Eventually, she presents the inspector with her ticket, crumpled and sorrowful. The inspector duly punches a large hole in the ticket and hands it back, smiling at Clara. He leans over and kisses her on the cheek.

'I'm going to fucking,' declares Mick, as he jumps into the air, rage all over his face. His fists are raised, his anger boiling over.

'Mick! Get a grip, will you!' The voice of his commander has spoken. Clara stretches out her hand and grabs Mick's arm. Her dainty hand cannot stretch all the way around her lover's arm.

'He fucking kissed you! That's fucking outrageous!'

Mick turns to Clara and me, his comment reverberating around the compartment. I try to repress and repress, but out it sneaks – a smirk appears on my face. Mick glowers at me. Pure unadulterated animosity. Mick's look of hatred just keeps reinforcing my smirk. Every time I try to think about anything else I just look at Mick's face, contorted and troubled.

'What you fucking smirking at? Some complete fucking stranger comes and fucking kisses your sister and you just sit there and smirk!'

Mick's anger is now directed at my demonstrable inability to stand up for myself, my lack of pride, my preparedness to let everyone walk all over me. I open my book and begin to read. Mick is incensed.

'Aren't you even going to... I don't know. Aren't you a man?'

More than you'll ever be, I tell myself.

WE ARE STANDING in a car park. To our right an imposing building casts a long shadow over us, blocking out the sun's rays. Mick is fiddling with his shoelaces. Clara is sitting on a wall studiously reading her guidebook. Ed looks lost in thought. He is without the prompt of an obscure work of philosophy today, but he doesn't need one. He wanders around, his head focused on the ground in front, as if he is worrying somebody has surreptitiously placed a tripwire or a landmine. He stops, looks to his left and his right, upwards towards the roof and walks away, away.

Ed begin to wander towards me, Mick asks him some-thing. Ed turns, his mood of contemplation shattered. Both stare at watches. Shoulders are shrugged. Nods in unison. Smiles abound. What are they talking about? Mick says something, Ed laughs. Mick laughs. I rise. I want to know the cause of such jollity. I walk over briskly and with purpose. The other two turn as they see me approach.

'What's the joke?'

'What?' Mick responds.

'What's the joke?' I repeat, my eyes flicking from Mick to Ed. Their expressions are still full of joy. 'Well, aren't you going to tell me?'

'Tell you what?' Ed answers in a matter-of-fact voice.

'What the joke is?'

'Nothing.'

'Yeah, nothing,' chimes in Mick.

These two obviously don't want me to know what they were talking about. Why? I get on well with both. Ed and I had a small difference of opinion in Warsaw. Mick and I, admittedly, had a small altercation in the train yesterday, but there is no underlying animosity. I look at both of them again. Neither is prepared to divulge the secret. I turn to walk back towards Clara. Laughter. Laughter. Mick and Ed are laughing at me. I turn sharply. 'Okay, guys you've had your little joke, now what's the secret?'

Shoulders are shrugged. Blank faces stare back at me. Ed and Mick have made a pact. They are not prepared to talk. They are not prepared to disclose their joke to me. The only possible reason for their silence is a joke at my expense. Very funny! Here I am, their guide, interpreter, the person who has been appointed official spokesman for the group – and these ungrateful sods decide to have a joke at my expense. That's gratitude for you. There have been many times on this journey when it would have been so much easier to have been alone. Supererogation. And for what?

The bus arrives. It is a special service organised by one of the expensive hotels. We had decided last night to take an organised trip. I was outvoted three to one, but after my debacle in Warsaw I gave in to the majority view. A group of Japanese tourists are sitting at the front. They look at us as we board. We go to the back of the bus away, out of sight, out of mind.

*

Clara is crying. Tears are streaming down her face and not even Mick's bear-hug seems able to comfort her. The display cabinet has a little caption in the bottom right-hand corner, but nobody needs an explanation. Piles upon piles of children's suitcases. They brought all the worldly belongings they could in those battered suitcases, but none returned. Ed is staring at a pile of human hair. It had been shaved off from the inmates' heads as they entered the camp and used to stuff pillows. *Arbeit Macht Frei.* Freedom from what? Freedom to do what? Free from thinking your own thoughts? Freedom to die without any dignity?

Our guide has walked on. She is rushing and rushing. She has probably been here many times before; she has probably become immune to all the horrific scenes. I just want to stand and wait, stand and hope to find an explanation.

'Please! Please!'

The guide is looking at the four of us and pointing at her watch.

'Sorry, we must go!'

I don't want to go, I don't want to leave. I want to stand here and think.

The bus takes us on to Auschwitz-Birkenau, the death camp. It is barren and desolate. The infamous railway line runs from the gate, the terminus beyond. I stand here, thinking, contemplating life, musing over my luck and good fortune. I may gripe and groan, but I have much to be pleased about. My culture, my ethnic group, my sexuality, my skin colour, my political beliefs are tolerated. I can live, those who came here were not allowed to.

Nobody speaks on the way back to Krakow. We are lost, deep in thought, deep in recollection.

W E LEAVE THE church just after two. The journey from the church will take us about half an hour. I attempt to engage Natasha in conversation, but she apologises and indicates her desire to rest.

'We have much partying to do.'

She arrived in London yesterday morning after a mammoth bus journey from Warsaw. No doubt Ed has kept her busy with energetic pursuits since she arrived in England. I allow my mind to wander, back to that journey, back to the train journey of such delight. Although I have travelled since that adventure, it still seems special. The bakery in Estonia, the café in St Petersburg, the swimming in Lithuania, the Chopin Museum in Warsaw, the twenty-four hour bar in Budapest and Radka in Prague.

I met Radka on a bridge. It all seemed so wonderfully metaphorical. I was walking from the western side of the city towards the centre. She was walking from the east. My gait was fast, as it is wont to be whenever I am alone. Besides, I wanted to explore the backstreets and immerse myself in Kafka's city. As I walked across the bridge, I was teasing myself with thoughts of the future. It was rosy. I had in front of me six months in Germany, six in Russia, another year in London. A warm glow of expectation enveloped my soul.

A T-shirt was moving towards me. It had a solitary word emblazoned upon it, cool. Its wearer had long black hair and a stunning body. The wearer was striding purposefully from the other side, anger palpable in every step. As she approached, tears were pouring down her cheeks. Why was someone so pretty, so attractive, so unhappy? Here I was, happy, joyous, gleeful, jocose, jubilant and yet a few steps away someone could be so unhappy. It all seemed so unfair.

A newspaper slipped from her grasp. A thud could be heard as it fell. She continued walking, oblivious to sight and sound. I started to move towards her, towards her newspaper. It was an English newspaper. It was a copy of *The Times*. I bent down, Clara's favourite expression ringing through my mind, 'Life's not a rehearsal. Life's not a rehearsal!' Trite, clichéd, but, Tom, come on! Come on!

I ran up to and just beyond her so I could turn to look at her.

'Excuse me!'

Her face turned towards mine. Her dark eyes, so large and sorrowful, looked at me. I stood there marvelling at those beautiful eyes. I was enraptured.

'Yes?' Her voice was so melodic. Or am I just imagining how melodic it was? How can one judge by just one word, just one syllable? Her tears had started to make her mascara run.

'You dropped your newspaper.'

I handed it over to her, my eyes refusing to move away from her voluptuous visage. She smiled. Another tear snaked down her face. She lifted her hand to her face in an attempt to hide her tear. I gulped.

'Would...' I pause, 'would you like to have a coffee or tea or something?'

A broad smile enveloped her face. Smiles engender smiles. Happiness engenders happiness.

We spent a wonderful afternoon sitting in the cafés of Prague chatting ceaselessly. The hordes of tourists being marched along the streets just passed me by. I was travelling along another street. My mind was not on the route, nor the direction, nor the destination, just on my travelling companion. I discovered she was a student of English and German. She wanted to go and live in America. She had been upset by her boyfriend, who'd told her she wasn't very good. I told her in all sincerity how good her English was. She smiled. 'You're just saying that,' she kept saying. It was good, not excellent, but aren't men allowed to exaggerate slightly when they want to spread a little happiness? I had certain ultimate objectives, but I am not totally cynical. Happiness spreads happiness.

Her charm worked its magic. My charm took much longer. I had been won over from the first glance. She had to be won over by mine. We walked through the backstreets of the city. I talked and talked. I talked about my life, my hopes for the future and recounted a couple of anecdotes from the journey. She laughed, she smiled, she radiated beauty. The evening ended in her small flat. We were horizontal all evening. I fell in love.

Friends have asked me since what she was like. There was the usual tangling of limbs, whispered sweet nothings and lots of sweat. But when one falls in love, marks out of ten do not run through one's mind. One does not think about instant reaction and analysis. Enjoyment, happiness, felicity. I was in love and I loved that evening.

'What's on your mind, mate?'

The music has stopped. Ed has both hands on the wheel, but his mind is elsewhere. He is looking across at me, desperate to know why a large, smug grin had crossed my face.

'I'm just thinking, you've got your Natasha here, I wonder where Radka is? Do you remember me talking about her?'

The mention of her name engenders a warm tingle in my heart.

'Frequently,' replies Ed.

He adds nothing. I remain silent, deep in my thoughts. The conversation, like the relationship with Radka, is short, but lost to the past.

B Y THE TIME Ed drives through the gates of the hotel most of the other guests have arrived. Natasha so quiet, so tranquil throughout the journey, suddenly springs to life. She rubs her hands with glee and begins to lavish elegant vocabulary. The setting could be described as 'picturesque', 'quaint' (although I despise the word because it implies one is looking down one's snooty nose) and 'charming'. Idyllic is stretching things a little too far, but her enthusiasm is welcome and infectious, even if her words aren't. She seems captivated by the tall gothic towers, the grand stone entrance.

We straighten our clothes and brush each other's backs. Ed helps Natasha to straighten her hat. They trade compliments. They exchange kisses. They stop and both turn their heads to look at me. I feel uncomfortable. Natasha grabs my left arm and wraps her right one around it. The three of us walk together to the entrance. She is beautiful, elegant and charming. How honoured I feel to walk into a wedding reception with such a beautiful woman on my arm. She may also have her arm around another man, she may be doing it out of a sense of friendship and fun, but boy do I hold my head high!

The hotel staff are moving quickly. They have perfected the art of rushing without looking like it. Bow ties and smiles skip quickly from side to side. They remain as elegant as swans, but they are frantically paddling. We are all ushered into the garden. The photographer stands waiting to seize the day. Alan and Mel are already there, arm in arm, grinning.

The photographs drag on and on and on. Alan and Mel standing this way, Alan and Mel standing that way, Alan and Mel sitting by a tree, Alan and Mel standing by the tree, Alan and Mel kissing, Alan and Mel with their parents standing this way. Mel's smile, one of the world's most ubiquitous phenomena, is beginning to wane. The assorted collection of guests is beginning to shuffle and fidget. Thumbs twiddle, dresses are adjusted, throats are cleared. The 'happy couple' mantra is wearing terribly thin. I feel hungry. How can I think such a thing at this time? In the church, my mind had no focus other than Natasha, now here at the reception, I can only think about my stomach. The hangover has passed, the stomach has recovered its voracious appetite. I'm hungry.

The waiters must be mind-readers. Balanced precariously on their outstretched palms, they bring canapés. Until now, I've always thought canapés were a stupid idea. They don't satisfy, they just augment hunger. My hunger is eased, however, by the thought that these canapés are the first little taster of the meal to come.

After waiting an inordinate amount of time, the photographer finally gets to number three hundred and thirty on his list, friends of the bride and groom. From the four corners of the garden, the friends make their way to the couple. We are a motley crew. Designer suits, cheap suits, silk ties, acrylic ties, earrings, nose-rings, Soho haircuts, backstreet haircuts, polished shoes, unpolished boots, straggly beards, shaven heads, red lipstick, purple lipstick. We do not make a pretty picture, but we are enthusiastic.

The food is wonderful, simple, straightforward, but wonderful. Who needs gourmet food, small portions of decorous cuisine, when one can have good honest grub? Tomato soup to start, meat and three veg and a strawberry cheesecake. I scoff the food and gulp the wine with equal gusto.

The tables have ten chairs placed around them. To my right, Ed is sitting with Natasha. Sue and Vlad the Mad are to their right. The other five chairs are taken by the previously unknown. There is a large jocular man called Jimmy McBride. He is an old friend of the bride's family. He insists on recounting to us in laborious detail his journey from Forfar. To his right sits a meek creature who introduces herself as Samantha. She adds nothing to the conversation, she just smiles whenever someone makes a good joke, while pushing the peas around her plate. To my left sits a couple, Liam and Sarah. They seem engrossed in themselves, unwilling to enter into any kind of conversation. Three couples, three private conversations, four remainders, leftovers in the coupling equation. I attempt to open up the discussion, but all my attempts rebound in my face. Jimmy, it turns out, is a quality controller. Sam just keeps mum.

The other member of the table is Kingchai, or at least that's what it sounds like. She is from Japan and her English isn't too extensive, so there is no chance to discuss the intricacies of Japanese politics or Japan's chances in the next World Cup. She is willing, however. At formal occasions, that's all I ever ask of people. I don't expect them to have the slightest interest in who I am, what I'm doing, or my opinion on the price of fish, but I want them to at least pretend. That's what I'm doing, nodding, as Kingchai tells me slowly, very slowly – snails are overtaking her – that she loves England. If I were in Japan I would be doing the same thing. Do unto others and all that.

A thud. Another thud. Another thud. A voice. 'Ladies and Gentlemen.' Mel's dad rises from his chair. He has clasped in his left hand a scrap or two of yellow paper. His hand is visibly shaking, imperceptible to those who have poured the potent red wine down their gullets, but I opted for beer. 'Thank you!' he exclaims. 'Thank you all for coming on this special day.' He looks down at his notes, raises his glass of water and sips the lubricant. 'I know many of you have travelled a long way. Some from Scotland.' Jimmy smiles and nods. 'Some from Spain, some from Japan.' Kingchai smiles. 'If we were to add all the miles together, Alan and Mel,' he turns towards the newly betrothed, 'that's a sign of how much we all love you.' Warm applause, cheers. Mel blushes, Alan mouths a thank-you to everyone. It may not have been a novel line. It may not even make much sense, but the old ones are such crowd-pleasers.

B UDAPEST STATION AT eleven thirty in the evening isn't the most warm and welcoming place on earth. Armed with just a guidebook and a head full of top tips for young travellers, we alight from the train. The procedure is routine. Our four rucksacks are heaped in a pile; two of us will stay with them and rest our weary heads while the other two try to find a map and some water.

Ed and I volunteer to go searching. The station, however, is dead. There is one man wandering around singing, with a bottle of beer in one hand and an unshaven face. All the kiosks and stores both inside and outside the building are shut. A map, a map, my rucksack for a map!

After what seems like fifteen minutes wandering around we resign ourselves to attempting to navigate the centre of Hungary's capital without the aid of a map, just a few incoherent lines in our guidebook.

We step outside on to the city streets. A couple of buses zoom past. Empty people-transporters full of light, but lacking in life. We have no idea which bus to take; the guidebook helpfully only informs us of the nearest metro station. It also divulges the useful information that the tube system closes down soon after eleven thirty. We have only one option, shank's pony.

Sweat is pouring off my back. It may be past midnight, but the city is hot. We are walking fast. We have a purpose.

We must look so conspicuous. Four people wearing rucksacks, carrying their lives on their backs like snails. Ed is leading us on. He has a hunch where we are supposed to go. He is determined to lead the troops. We are happy to follow the self-declared sergeant major. It is too late to argue, too late to quibble. We just want to find somewhere, find somewhere to rest our weary heads.

We walk past a huge stone square on the right. It looks like something out of classical antiquity. I begin to wander towards it, my natural curiosity egging me on.

'Where are you going?' Ed shouts.

I turn like a startled rabbit.

'What are you doing? I know it looks very interesting, but it's already past midnight, we haven't got anywhere to stay, the hostel is still miles away. What the fuck are you doing?'

I turn. Mick is crouching down tying his right shoelace. Clara has in her left hand a bar of chocolate and her right is on Ed's shoulder. I shrug my shoulders. I have no logical explanation and wander back towards the rest of the group.

Ed leads us on through the quiet streets. We twist and turn, left and right. My mind wanders. I think of salt and vinegar crisps, of Liverpool's chances next season, of whether Hawaiian or Sicilian is my favourite flavour of pizza. My legs, however, are autonomous, they are just following Ed's. Left, right, left, right, left.

'Right. Here we are!'

I look up. In front of my face are four or five steps; they lead to a door, an unpromising door. Nothing seems to be visible. I point at the door. My finger and my expression ask whether this is the right place. Clara shrugs her shoulders. Ed nods.

'Someone else can do all the sweet-talking. Step forward Mr Linguistic.'

I open the door. I feel like a small, hungry child opening a fridge. Light hits my face. It augurs well.

'Have you got any space for four people?'

My voice contains a hint of desperation. The girl shakes her head. She glances at her book, looks at the clock.

'Look, it's after midnight. Why don't you put your rucksacks in the', she stops and searches her mind for the right word, 'lockers over there. Go downstairs. There is a nonstop bar downstairs. Maybe there will be a bed free by six.'

I stop for a second. This hostel owner is imploring me to party the night away, to dance, to sing, to drink. I am not going to complain. After the day's journey we have just endured, I need a drink. We step slowly down the steps towards the bar. Loud, energetic music is booming out of the room. We turn the corner.

There in front of us is a room of hedonism. I turn towards Ed, throw my arms into the air and exclaim, 'Yes!'

*

Today has been a difficult and turbulent day. It all started so well. We got to Krakow station at around seven thirty. We were on our way to Bucharest, to Romania, but we ended the day in Budapest. Ed and Mick sat on the platform munching doughnuts and sipping hot coffee. I walked up and down the platform, stretching my legs, before we began our journey into the unknown. Clara studied the guidebook, occasionally sharing some of her gems.

The train eased itself into the station and we eased ourselves aboard, making a compartment in the third carriage our little nest. The compartment door was flung open. A short woman dressed in a blue uniform was standing there, a ticket puncher in her left hand. I passed over a ticket. She put a series of holes in it and then asked for something.

'*Billet, Fahrkarten*, ticket.' I looked at Ed. He shrugged his shoulders. She repeated her statement.

'I don't understand,' I said and showed her the piece of paper again.

'This is not ticket.'

I stared at her in disbelief.

'What is that?' Ed asked, pointing at the paper in my hand, his diction simple, his delivery slow and pointed.

'It is for seat, not go!' she replied, her glance shifting from Ed's to mine. She wanted one of us to understand.

'What's the matter'?' asked Mick, his face questioning and contorted.

Ed sighed.

'That wonderful deal we got at the station. Four dollars for a trip to Bucharest. Well, we bought a seat reservation; it wasn't a ticket for the journey.'

'Bollocks,' replied Mick. In just one word, he managed to encapsulate all our thinking.

'What we going to do? We can't afford that,' he added, looking towards me, the oracle. I shrugged my shoulders.

Ed looked towards the ticket inspector whose eyes had been watching the verbal tennis game. Her face suggested she understood nothing.

'We were told this ticket was a ticket for the journey, not just a seat reservation.'

She wouldn't budge. To be fair, the difference between a ticket and a seat reservation was a very substantial amount of money. We agreed to pay for new tickets, although she could only issue us with tickets to the border. All our Polish money had been spent in a groovy café the night before. How I longed to return to that haven of dancing, singing and beer swilling! I had overexerted myself in the café. I kept consoling myself, I would have hours to rest on the train on the following day. It was not to be. The next twenty minutes were spent bargaining, calculating, recalculating, reasoning, discussing, checking the recalculation until we were agreed how many dollars equalled the requisite number of *zloty*. In consequence, I had no time to relax and reflect on the Polish experience.

A sense of foreboding gripped all four of us as we approached the Polish-Slovak border. We knew our ticket was only valid until the border. We had no Slovak money. Would we be forcibly ejected from the train? The four of us sat and gazed out of the window, no one said anything to anyone. Periodically, eyes would wander, but whenever eyes met, they quickly moved apart. We were scared of eye contact. Everyone in their own way was culpable. We had all bought the tickets together. Ed admittedly had spoken to the woman at the desk, but we were all behind him, both metaphorically and literally.

Mick was the most agitated. After the Pinteresque silence had lasted for around half an hour, he rose from his seat.

'Why didn't you check the ticket, Ed? Why?'

His finger pointed at Ed's forehead. An accusational arrow aimed straight at Ed's cerebral organ. Ed sighed and looked away. Mick stood there unflinching and repeated the accusation.

'Why didn't you check the ticket, Mick? All the decisions always come down to us.' He pointed at me, to indicate I was included in the *us*. 'If you didn't like the decision, you could've said something, but you didn't. Yes, I made a mistake. I will stand up and admit my failings, but you, you just sit,' he saw Mick's upright bodily position, 'or stand and moan. Besides, if it weren't for us, you wouldn't even be here. If it weren't for us, you'd be sitting in your local just having a beer. We've broadened your mind, shown you things you'd never have done on your own. And do you appreciate it? No, you just moan. Moan about money, about us, about every fucking thing.'

Clara rises.

'Look, guys. We fucked up. We're all stupid. Let's just cool it. Okay.'

Mick nodded, Ed nodded, I nodded. The voice of reason had spoken. Silence was returned.

★

I negotiated the Slovak ticket collectors with relative ease. The young inspector seemed a mite baffled by the situation, but after consulting his boss, we were allowed to proceed. Persuasion was needed to convince the inspectors to take dollars. A little sense and sensibility on both sides sorted it all out. Ed took a back seat and read his novels.

Silence still reigned until the train pulled into Košice. Ed put down his Jane Austen and transported himself into another time zone. He stood up. He gazed out through the lenses of his golden glasses. He stood there motionless. The other three of us were distracted by the hustle and bustle of those getting on and those getting off. Ed remained motionless, his gaze focused on a distant point in time and space.

He turned, his face grave and solemn. He lifted his hand to his chin and cleared his throat. We all looked at him in expectation of a great announcement. Perhaps Ed had solved one of the great questions of the universe.

'Mick, Clara, Tom.' He looked at each of us as he said our names. He continued, his words full of *gravitas*, 'I don't think we should carry on.'

He sat down. Was he advocating suicide? Or just suggesting we remain in Košice?

'What?'

Clara looked at him in utter astonishment, sheer disbelief.

'What do you mean? Do you want to visit this town, what's it called?' Clara began to flick through her guide-book. 'Is there something worth seeing here? 'What do you mean?'

'There is no point continuing,' responded Ed, turning back towards the window.

Clara couldn't take any more; she was completely baffled. She didn't know what to do, or what to say. She stood up and began to pace the compartment, agitation radiating from every step.

'No point continuing where?' she bellowed, desperation in her voice. 'What are you talking about?'

Clara seemed visibly shaken. Ed had said a few words and yet with those few words he had turned a tranquil scene into something sepulchral. A melancholy air had descended so quickly. Ed's voice, its crisp elegant enunciation of the words, seemed to carry authority.

'There is no point carrying on to Bucharest.'

Ed's answer was so undramatic and yet so dramatic. He had said nothing unusual in terms of his choice of words, but his tone carried everything and yet nothing.

'I suggest we take this train to the Hungarian border and take a train to Budapest and forget Bucharest.'

His voice was authoritative.

We all assented without demurring. Inert masses responding to their master's voice.

D ISCO. DISCO INFERNO. D.I.S.C.O. The disco part of the day's festivities has begun. Everyone joins in. Mel's granny has decided to display her dancing prowess to all who care to watch. She has been goaded on to the dance floor by three of her grandchildren, desperate to see this woman, who has often spoken about her dancing prowess, particularly her second place in the 1947 Bournemouth tango trophy. She doesn't move particularly quickly, but more disturbing is her utter lack of a sense of rhythm. She seems incapable of moving with the beat. She must have been blessed with a talented partner in those halcyon days.

Robert Smythe hasn't got a sense of rhythm either, but he has got a goal, dancing closer and closer, hinting, probing, winking, nodding, suggesting. The object of his desires is a short plump girl called Tabatha. She reminds me of a cat. Her head is raised and proud. Despite her height she attempts to stare down the barrel of her nose at all who show an interest, including, and especially, Robert.

Sitting at one of the tables to my right Jimmy continues to retell all within earshot about his journey to the wedding. Kingchai continues to listen. Periodically, she laughs, rolls her head back and emits a chuckle or a guffaw. Most of the time, however, a frown rules her face. She cannot understand a word Jimmy says. His broad Scottish accent gives Kingchai no chance. Samantha just sits there. She doesn't need to listen. Repetition adds nothing.

The atmosphere changes. The mood swings. There is an exodus from the dance floor. All the single men and single women return to their chairs, or pretend they are desperate for another drink or the toilet – nothing to do with the fact the DJ has decided to spin a romantic record. All the wild and reckless dancers leave. The dance floor is left in the safe hands of the couples. The rest of us sit in our chairs anxious to return. We don't want to sit, we want to dance. The couples are fortunate, they can disperse to the four corners of the room and osculate. The remainder, those who cannot fit into neat social equations, just wait. I exchange smiles with a few other single people, but no matter how hard our friends try, we aren't interested in the other singles in the room, we just want to dance. Let's dance.

Relief. The DJ realises that romantic songs, like brutal dictatorships, just cause those who can't sing along to flee. He puts on some Beatles. Safe, reliable and popular. They flood back, the small boy too ashamed to ask his older imposing cousin, those with no self-esteem, those with too much self-esteem, those frankly not interested in anyone here and those who just want to dance. We are the life and soul of the disco. Let us dance!

After dancing away to the Beatles, Blondie, Bowie and Blur I return to my seat, sweat pouring off my brow. I search in my pocket for a handkerchief, to mop my glistening forehead. Both Ed and Natasha fumble in their pockets. Natasha finds a tissue and gives it to me. How kind. Ed's face displays concern. He continues to fumble.

'I think I've left my house keys in the car. I must go and get them, otherwise I'll worry all night.'

Still fumbling in his pocket, he rises from his chair.

'D'you mind if I join you? I'm in need of a breath of fresh air.'

I stretch.

'Sure,' Ed says, turning to Natasha. 'You don't mind waiting here for a bit, do you?'

Natasha smiles and winks.

'Good day, isn't it!' I comment, as we walk out of the hotel towards the car park.

'It's been a wonderful day. I love weddings, but this wedding is special. This is the first wedding I've ever been to when I've had a beautiful woman on my arm! Isn't she wonderful!'

Ed looks towards me; he wants me to offer him my seal of approval. I smile, nod, throw my hand in the air, open my mouth and shake my head. What should one say in such circumstances? Men want their partners to be considered very attractive propositions, but not that attractive. Enough to turn heads and to get people talking about her, not enough to lust after her.

'How come you've never spoken about her?'

'I was always very keen on her, but I always thought she wasn't that interested in me.' He pauses as he tumbles under the seats. Those keys are proving to be elusive. 'She', he continues, 'didn't respond to many of my letters.' He sighs, 'I can't understand, I just don't understand, where my keys are. I had them at the church. I had them.'

'Did I tell you the big news in the Reed family?'

'No.' Ed is ferreting around in the boot of his car.

'Mick and Clara may not be getting married. All plans are on hold. They had a huge row about something. No one knows the exact reason, but the upshot is that, well, there ain't gonna be a wedding.'

Ed lifts his head out of the boot. He looks at me. A look of pure astonishment gazes at me. Ed seems incapable of saying anything, he just frowns. His body language asks the question.

'Clara, apparently, has accused Mick of holding back secrets from her.'

'Like what?'

'I think you know.'

I look at Ed. The sun is beginning to set. His gold-rimmed spectacles are all I can see clearly, his eyes, half-visible, seem to be hiding. 'Ed, what happened on the train between Budapest and Vienna?'

'Look, mate, we are at a wedding. It's been a great day, why ruin it?'

He slams the car door and begins to walk back to the hotel. I run after him. My tie flies over my shoulder. I am panting, but I manage to shout, 'Ed, my sister may be marrying Mick, why can't you tell me what happened on that train journey? My sister may end up spending the rest of her life with this man. I,' I pause for breath, 'I need to know. My sister deserves to know.'

Ed stops.

'Sometimes, Tom, certain things are best left as mysteries.'

'Come on, Ed! You're not going to fob me off again, are you? Can't you just tell me what happened? Was it *that* bad?'

Ed remains motionless. He doesn't respond, he doesn't say anything. He doesn't make a move.

'It *was* bad, wasn't it?'

Ed's face offers no reaction.

'Ed, look I have a right to know. There is a right to know!'

'Stop donning your fucking journalist cap! You've read Ibsen's *The Wild Duck,* your favourite fucking play. You know sometimes the discovery of truth causes more heartache than if everything has remained swept under the carpet.'

Why is Ed ranting on about Ibsen? We are not talking about a doll's house, we are talking about my sister.

Ed storms back towards the car, he has realised he still hasn't found his keys.

'Ed!' I shout loudly and run after him. 'Ed, I appreciate you don't want to tell me, but you know I'm not going to let this one go now. I can't. It relates to my sister.'

Ed stops. He puts his hands on his hips and turns his head skyward, his back still facing me. He seems to be looking for a line, an explanation. His head remains transfixed by something in the heavens.

'Tom, please take this the right way. We are good mates. I've told you many of my deepest darkest secrets. I've told you things I wouldn't tell anybody else, not even my future wife, but there are certain things you don't need to know. Look...' Ed turns and stares at me. The light from the hotel's bright security lamp lights up his face. 'Look...' he repeats, a hint of desperation has crept into his voice. 'Look...' Ed, a man who normally has no problem stringing together coherent sentences, seems unable to articulate his thoughts. He looks at me and opens his mouth. As he begins to speak, his head sinks; its focal point is no longer my face, but a solitary stone on the ground. 'Can't you just leave it out?' He moves forward, kicks the stone and walks away.

Part Six

Towards the Centre

S MILE TOM. SMILE. I hate networking and false amity, but sometimes one has to prostitute one's desires to achieve one's ends.

'Hi Lizzy!'

Lizzy is tall and elegant. I've met her a few times before. She works in the conference department.

'Oh, hi Tom!'

She looks up from her desk laden with paperwork; only her face peeps over the defences. She knows I want something from her. Nobody in business is charming unless they want something from you. We exchange a 'How are you?' Both of us reply with a trite platitude.

'I hear you're organising a conference in Vienna,' I say, dispensing with the unsatisfactory *hors d'oeuvre* and begin to chomp through the meat and two veg. She nods. She seems reluctant to provide me with a tasty sauce.

'Lizzy, I've got the Polish PM's office on the line,' a voice screams across the room.

Lizzy smiles, holds up her index finger to indicate the expected length of the call and grabs her receiver. Meal interrupted. I gaze around the room. To my left, is a diminutive woman desperately turning her computer on and off and cursing the advent of modern technology. To my right, a pair of braces is sweet-talking someone on the phone. Promises of delights, of top-billing, of untold riches.

'Sorry about that, Tom,' says Lizzy, as she returns the receiver to its proper home. 'Yes, I'm putting together a little jamboree in a month's time.'

She passes me a copy of the agenda and watches me as I glance down the list of speakers and topics. My eye catches sight of the names of three prime ministers, three central bank governors and other crowd-pullers.

'Very impressive.'

'I've got and about four hundred delegates coming.'

Her voice is not too loud, but it is piercing. Everyone in her department knows her success, but she just wants to make sure. Her colleagues do not seem that impressed, however. No heads turn, no one flinches. The audience has forgotten the script, they have forgotten to clap.

*

I open the door. The sight of a sea of suits greets me. Loud ties and pints of lager are omnipresent. Deals, anecdotes and conquests fill the air. The pair of braces I saw earlier today is leaning on the bar, a red fiery dress the object of his desire. His voice is loud and confident, his speech banal and unimpressive. The dress is desperate to inch away, but she is hemmed in. The bar is full.

'Oh, hi, Tom!'

It's Lizzy. She has plastered her face with more make-up. She is surrounded by men. Eager to talk, eager to try it on. Now she has a willing audience.

'Tom,' she grabs my arm, 'this is Arthur.' I exchange nods with a tall black-haired man, who has a terrible spot on his face. He is cheerful and probably harbours hopes of docking at Lizzy's port this evening. His red blemish will preclude that. I haven't the heart to tell him. Besides it would be cruel and he might have a violent turn.

'This is Max. He works in marketing.' I smile a truly false smile. 'And this is another Tom, he works in advertising.'

'When I was in Moscow, last week,' Max announces. Just in case we did not hear correctly he repeats the location of his recent sojourn. 'It was fucking awful, the Russians are such corrupt fucking wankers. They overcharged me for everything, the bastards.'

His Etonian accent is grating enough, using swear words to make himself look hard is pathetic, but what really engenders my bile is his anti-Russian nonsense.

'Do you speak Russian?' I ask.

'*Nyet*,' he exclaims and bursts out laughing.

The others raise a smile, but do not emit a noise. I ponder for a second and then decide not to pursue the argument. He is a lost cause.

'Tell me more about Vienna, Lizzy.' I enquire, knowing the female member of our group will love to tell everyone what a wonderful conference she is putting together.

The tape recorder was all set, now the play button is depressed and off she goes recounting the libretto. She knows how to work an audience. She lays stress on all the right words, litters her speech with jokes and aphorisms and moves her head periodically to look straight into our eyes, the chosen ones. Max laughs the loudest and longest. Every time he emits a laugh, a chortle, a guffaw, Lizzy smiles. She's only encouraging him, enticing him on. How she loves to play with mere mortals.

SAUSAGES. DON'T ASK me why, but I cannot stop thinking about sausages. Sausages and lashings of hot mustard. Fortunately, the airport terminal has a restaurant that serves a lame impression of an all-day breakfast, not one of those all-day breakfasts that one can buy in the heart of South London. The plate isn't even full. The solitary sausage and egg are on opposite sides of the plate and a white chasm of empty china reflects the light from the strip lights back on to my face.

Time is ticking by. My plane to Prague will depart in two hours' time. As usual I completely misjudged how long it would take to get from my house to Heathrow. Last night, I was kept awake, wondering whether there would be a strike, or a mechanical fault, or a bomb scare, or some such reason why the tube wouldn't be running. I decided to base my time calculations on the assumption that the journey would have to be taken by bus. But if there was a problem with the tube more people would have to travel by bus or car, the roads would be jammed. An extra thirty minutes would be necessary. In the end, I took a sleeping pill and fell asleep, dreams of central Europe filling my shut-eye.

Radka has invited me to Prague. Or rather, if truth be told, I engineered an invitation. I have exchanged the occasional letter with her over the last few years. I wrote to her and told her I would be in Vienna on business and would like to spend a few days in Bohemia.

Summer 1994 seems so long ago now. Both the city and Radka are bound to have changed. I reach inside my coat pocket and take out my wallet. In among the plethora of friends' business cards, books of stamps and a rather crumpled leisure centre card, I find a photo of Radka. She doesn't look that beautiful. Am I making a big mistake? We haven't seen each other for two and a half years. I only spent one night with her all those years ago, now I'm planning to see her for two, maybe three. She may have cropped her hair, had her nose pierced, or joined a fascist group. Her letters had got shorter and shorter, until, that is, I wrote to her to tell her of my travel plans.

'Excuse me,' an Italian accent says to me.

I turn my head and smile. 'Eeee... do you know... where is gate number twelve?'

The accent belongs to a tanned man in an opened-necked shirt, a medallion hanging around his neck. He smiles, nods his head and enquires again.

'I'm terribly sorry,' my accent goes all BBC World Service, 'I don't know, but try asking that man over there in the blue suit and the cap.' I point at a man whose attire suggests he is an official of some description.

'Thank you, thank you,' the Italian responds, an effulgent smile on his face. He wanders over to the blue suit who starts to point and give him directions.

★

I stand by the luggage pick-up point. To my left, a football team clad in matching tracksuits are smiling and joking. To my right, a couple is arguing.

'What are you doing? Don't put that in there!' The heavily built male is berating his partner.

'Look, I did all the bloody packing!' she answers loudly.

Faces in the mêlée turn towards the couple. They become self-conscious. Their cheeks turn crimson. Their arguing ceases. The man uses the ensuing quiet to slip his hand into the small rucksack and take out the offending item. The woman, who is trying desperately to look around the terminal to give any observer the impression that her mind is wandering, hears the rustling and exclaims in a very loud whisper, 'John, please leave it in there. Everyone is watching us.' How true.

My battered brown suitcase, handed down the generations, comes into view. It trundles along towards me, sandwiched between two identikit bags belonging to the football players. They stretch out their arms ready to lift the sacks from the carousel. My arm is gradually extending, my hand ready to pounce. The footballers push forward and force me to one side. They see my arm is making a move towards their belongings. I receive a sharp pain in the side.

I step back and allow the two thugs to collect their precious bags. My suitcase will have to make another circuit of the carousel. It is a well-travelled suitcase. Another lap will not trouble it unduly. Besides, I don't feel in the mood to take on the might of the football team. I may have been blessed with a fine right jab, but a punch can only hit one thug at one time. Moreover, Radka is waiting for me somewhere. I don't want to her to meet me in prison.

I walk out through the automatic doors into Prague airport. I have arranged to meet Radka in the centre of the city, but I still hold out hope she will be at the airport. I look to the left. I look to the right. I look back to the left. She isn't here. Perhaps she doesn't love me.

I walk over to one of the seats next to the window and take out her crumpled letter from my pocket and begin to read:

Dear Tom,

*I am very happy you are coming to Prague. It will be good
fun, I have a surprise for you. I cannot meet you at the airport, please come to house of my parents, I have written
directions for you on the back of this letter...*

I follow her instructions. Bus to Dejvicka number 119. The
bus is full. I am forced to stand. Sitting to my right is a
couple. She is short with a pale face and a petite nose. He
has earrings and stubble. They are in each other's arms,
caressing each other and whisperings promises of undying
love. In front of me is a burly man, a large rucksack on his
back with several badges sown on to it. Pride of place is a
Canadian flag. He turns round and smiles at me. He must
have eyes in the back of his head.

'Hi!' he exclaims, while raising his right hand as if he is
about to swear allegiance.

'Hello,' I reply tentatively. 'You've flown in from Can-
ada, have you?'

'Nope, I was in London, I'm on a European tour.'

His voice seems to be getting louder and louder. Necks
are turning, faces are glaring. I pause, wondering whether
to continue the conversation, but the traveller is a jovial
man who means well.

'How long are you going to spend in Prague?'

'Few days.' He can see the suits I'm carrying. 'You, here
on, er, business?'

'No,' I reply, 'I'm just here to visit some old friends.'

The bus swerves. The passengers are reshuffled. Instead
of the Canadian, an old lady is in front of me mumbling
and grumbling in a language I neither know nor care to
attempt to decipher. Her frail frame enables me to look
around the bus. My God! There, at the front of the bus, is a
grey-haired man, with round glasses and a beard. He looks

just like Dr Alan McDonald, one of my old university teachers. Dr McDonald was widely regarded as the star of the university Russian department. He had been snapped up by Harvard, or Yale, or somewhere, I thought. It would be rude not to say hello. He was always very civil and charming to me, but he wouldn't remember an insignificant plonker like me.

I am however hemmed in at the moment. The frail old lady is desperately clutching a pole with both her bony hands. If I ask to squeeze by she will probably lose her grip and fall to the floor. Besides, the Canadian man will interpret any movement up the bus on my part as an indication I want to talk to him.

Although the bus stops many times, all the passengers are waiting for the terminus. Awaiting them there is the luxury of the metro which will whisk all and sundry speedily towards their destinations. The bus speeds past row after row of tall white apartment blocks, homogenous and impersonal. Architects have much to answer for. Whatever Keynes said about the influence of dead economists and political thinkers, the worst legacy of the Communist period in Central and Eastern Europe are the buildings.

We arrive. The frail old lady's relief is palpable. She emits a smile and starts to push past me towards the door. The lovey-dovey couple have finished their cuddling and rise from their seat eager to spread the joyous news of their love on a different bus.

I get off and wait by the door. Out they pour, rucksacks, suitcases, holdalls, all shapes and sizes, of every conceivable colour and pattern. I spot the brown briefcase I've seen before on the front desk of a lecture theatre in London. The beard and the glasses look heavenward, but the briefcase points directly at me.

I clear my throat ostentatiously, but still the gaze is drawn to the sky.

'Dr McDonald.'

The gaze shifts towards the calling sound. A curious, quizzical look is replaced by a look of recognition when he lays his eyes on me. He stretches out his hand.

'Hello. Well, this is a surprise.' He is searching his mind for my name. He probably cannot quite place the face in front of him. 'What are you doing here?' he asks, as he wafts his hand around motioning towards the buildings around. He is playing for time, desperately ferreting around in his memory for the clue to the identity of the youth standing before him.

'I'm in Prague to see friends.' As soon as the words leave my lips I realise I'm not helping him to place me. 'I met them when I studied in Moscow in my year off.' Lie, lie, little white lie.

'Ah, yes.' A momentary pause and then he begins to speak quickly. 'Have you got a Tolstoy in your bag now or have you read them all by now? That was a good class: you, David, Phillipa, Andrew, Maria and Jarmila. So, Tom, where do your Bohemian friends live? I'm meeting some colleagues in a café just off the Old Town Square. I'm here for a symposium on semantics. Should be fun!' He clicks his fingers in front of his face and points at me. 'You are a good friend of Ed, what's his surname, Bailey, isn't it?' I can't remember, you know the one, he took my course *Ideas in Nineteenth Century Russian Literature,* did very well especially considering he couldn't speak Russian. Got eighty per cent in the exam. Well, last time I was in this part of the world, in Vienna actually, I bumped into him. I remember he was looking rather the worse for wear. Shame, he was going to take my course on the philosophy of Tolstoy, the one you did, was very keen. He didn't seem very chatty, something in the Viennese air must have changed his mind. God, that's a few years ago now. Only been to Russia and the US in the meantime. Bloody expensive travel these days. How's he doing?'

'Fine.'

'Good. Well, I must be off. Late already. Have a good time with your friends. See you, bye.' With that, the beard, glasses and battered academic briefcase disappear into the distance.

I reach into my pocket and begin to read the instructions. Radka has thoughtfully sketched a map on the reverse side of the letter. I wander up the street to the right. Her writing is so small I can't make out the name. My gaze begins to travel up the buildings. I don't want to stop and stand like a dummy on the street corner, I want to walk, to give the impression to any casual observer that I know where I am going and what I'm doing. I wander up the street, but something feels wrong. There is supposed to be a Chinese restaurant somewhere round here. Where the hell is it?

I notice an old lady carrying her shopping in a dark-green bag, a walking stick stuck in her right hand. I walk towards her smiling, desperate to catch her eye. I have tried to learn some Czech to impress Radka, but what with work and... Stop making excuses, Tom, just have a stab. The choice of verb disturbs me. Maybe the ghost of Patrick Bateman stalks my mind.

'Prosím.' I wonder whether that's the right word. The old lady looks up at me, her eyes narrow, her nose points at my face. She mumbles something incomprehensible. 'Prosím,' I repeat. What's the phrase for 'Where is,' 'Nevíte, kde je?' I point at the address at the top of Radka's letter. The eyes broaden, a finger settles on the tip of the nose. Up goes the finger pointing skyward. Down it comes and makes a curved movement as if it's stirring an invisible pot of something. The old lady is saying something. I've fallen into the oldest trap for travellers. Speak a few words of the natives' language out of courtesy and they assume you are fluent.

I eventually realise, after she's stirred the imaginary pot a thousand times, she is telling me to go back and up the next street virtually parallel to this one.

I follow her instructions and find the street. In front is a brown door. The number is correct. Radka's surname is there, third from the top, I hesitate. Suitcase in hand, I step back and look up. Am I making a mistake? I met her once all those years ago. Who am I kidding? I am trying to recapture a moment, admittedly a beautiful moment, which has past. She's probably changed. She even told me in her letter what she will be wearing. That disturbed me. She thinks I won't recognise her or something. I've agreed to meet her at her house and she feels the need to tell me what she will be wearing.

I rub my eyes vigorously, run my fingers through my hair, clear my throat and step forward and depress the bell.

It rings.

'Halo.' The voice is deep and masculine.

'Hello. Um, Tom here, is Radka there?'

I can hear two people by the intercom. A reply is shouted: something like 'Dare'.

'Radka.'

'No.'

Shit. This can't be her house. I look at the letter again, I look at the address, I look at the map. This must be the house. I sit down on my suitcase and rub my face with my hands. My watch beams back five o'clock. Maybe she doesn't want to see me. I should still have enough time to find somewhere else to stay. A chill wind blows down the street. Flakes of snow pirouette, dance down the street. Their partners whisk them from side to side and round and round.

'Tom.'

I look round. There she is. Looking beautiful. She kisses me on both cheeks, not on the mouth. An indication or just a precaution, I wonder.

'I thought you weren't here.'

'What? You asked for me and my dad said, "Yes". I was in the toilet.'

'But he said, "No".'

She laughs, but puts her two delicate hands towards her face to cover her glee.

'Tom, In Czech "*no*" is short for "*ano*" which means "yes".'

I feel stupid. I should have learnt that. It's probably on the next page of *Teach Yourself Czech*.

R ADKA STILL LIVES with her parents in their small, cluttered flat. They are not the dream liberal parents I was hoping for. Instead of allowing me to sleep in the same room as their daughter, they have borrowed some blankets from next door and offered me the sofa.

I cannot sleep. They were generous hosts. Bottles and bottles of Moravian wine were poured down our gullets while we ate dumplings and some meat. My head is spinning and I'm desperate for the Gents. I've already been to the toilet twice tonight. The flush is so loud. Niagara Falls must make less noise. I'm sure I've woken up the whole apartment block every time I've pulled the chain. I've been lying here thirty minutes hoping my waters will filter back up to my kidneys.

The door to Radka's room opens. A mass of long dark hair peers out. A smile greets me. She tiptoes over towards me, her nightdress long and flowing. She plants a kiss on my cheeks while running her fingers through my hair.

'Can't you sleep?' she whispers. I shake my head. She smiles, kisses me on the cheek and adds, 'Don't worry, you can sleep during the day tomorrow.'

She gets up and wanders into the bathroom. Two minutes later it's Niagara in the bathroom. She skips back to her bedroom, blowing me a kiss, towards my cheek, I'm sure.

★

I am woken by Niagara again. This time light is pouring through the window. Radka's dad is ready for his day's work. He works at one of the ministries. He is only a minor official, but seems content. 'I work seven thirty morning to three thirty afternoon,' he told me yesterday. 'It very good. I like to go to my cottage many times.'

I trade my horizontal posture for a vertical one. He raises his cup of coffee to salute my awakening. He points at his blue tie dangling down from his neck and announces, 'I go work.' He repeats, 'I go work. Good day.' With that promulgation he puts down his half-finished cup on the coffee table and walks towards the door, he waves his hand and adds like a three year old child a 'bye bye'.

Radka's mum told me last night she leaves home before her husband. I wander through to the kitchen, poke my head in to the bathroom and stand by the open door to the master bedroom. No one appears to be there. I knock on the door just in case. No answer. I enter. No one is there. Yes. I creep towards Radka's door and open it. I am aroused, I have been thinking, dreaming, rehearsing this for months. She is asleep. Her eyes are closed. Her face is poking itself above the duvet. I bend down. My lips are protruding, her cheek is my target. Bullseye.

Her eyes open. Her hand reaches out and touches my face. I start to kiss her neck. She turns her face towards mine. She kisses me on the lips. She runs her hand along my bare arm.

'Have my parents left already?'

'Yes.'

She pulls me on to her bed.

R ADKA LEADS ME through the streets of Prague. So much seems to have changed. I was here only two and a half years ago and yet everything seems to have changed. Last time I was here there were plenty of tourist shops and signs in English, but now they proliferate. Hot dogs, burgers, T-shirts, music, change. The bookshops even put up a sign to say 'Books'.

We walk hand in hand, but she's the master and I'm the dog. She drags me to the left and to the right, through small alleyways and across busy streets. We stop periodically for coffee, but her energy is boundless; she constantly wants to move onwards towards nowhere in particular. I just revel in the ride.

We take a tram that snakes its way up the side of the hill to the west of the Vltava River. We stand at the back and watch the magical city appear and disappear through the trees that line the route. I pull Radka in closer, in tight. I'm desperate to hang on to this moment.

'Okay. We get off here. Okay.'

There is no time for me to assent to her proposal. A sharp tug of the hand drags me from my moment of reflection.

An old blind man taps his white stick along the tram as Japanese tourists click their shutters. He reaches out for the pole. Before I have a chance to react, a friendly native helps him down the step and off the tram. I wanted to help, honestly, but I don't want to let Radka go.

'I have a surprise for you.'

She opens her bag and takes out an envelope. She passes it to me, I put my hand inside. I sport a worried frown. This is not the surprise I was expecting. I was hoping the surprise would entail a few softly spoken words, those well-worn three. I take out the bundle. Photographs. Photographs from the journey with Ed, Clara and Mick. I look at Radka inquisitively, my head angled at forty-five degrees, my left eyebrow climbing up my forehead.

'You left the film in the flat that night. You were in such a hurry.'

'I don't remember.' Why would I remember a poxy film when I had a beautiful woman and had a train to catch?

'Who are the people on the photos?'

'That is Ed, that's my sister, Clara, and that's Mick.'

Mick is standing with his top off and waving at the camera. His wrists pointing into the lens, he looks so happy. Probably has had a beer or two.

OUR RELATIONSHIP WILL continue on the same ambiguous footing. I've enjoyed the last forty-eight hours in Prague, enjoyed every moment so much that I haven't dared raise the question so loved by soap operas, 'Where is our relationship going?' I don't want it to go anywhere. Everything is wonderful as it is. Why does it have to travel on somewhere else? Why can't it stay still? Because I have to go to Lizzy's conference in Vienna, my job, my profession, my future. As much as I like to think of myself as an incurable romantic, I am too ambitious to just enjoy. I always want more.

Prague's main station isn't the most romantic place on earth, but it's where my brief encounter has to end. I have my train ticket, my battered suitcase and even the film. I have everything and yet something is being left behind. It feels strange as I stand on the platform. I have stood on so many platforms. So many trains have been boarded. Every single one has had its destination clearly marked on the front and I let it take me there or in that general direction. I have never stood on a platform ready to board and suddenly changed my mind, refused point-blank to be transported. As I hold Radka in my arms, I wonder whether I should break out, take my chance and be spontaneous.

Whistles, doors slamming, farewells, fill the air. Radka pulls her head back, plants a kiss on my lips and wishes me a good journey.

'Send me a postcard, please.'

'Sure.'

She pushes me on the train. I am not in control. She blows a kiss, she waves, she smiles, she laughs. How can she be so happy? I feel miserable. The end is nigh.

THE SNOW IS falling, flakes flutter in the wind. I am content; a pot of tea, a plateful of cakes, Viennese cakes, and a copy of the *Guardian*, what more could a man wish for? The piano player's fingers have started to dance around on the keyboard. *Summertime*. Play it again, Sam.

The conference begins tomorrow morning at nine. I have an afternoon to potter, think and drink tea. Various dignitaries may start to arrive during the evening, but I do not feel like interviewing them tonight. Charles told me earlier today to talk to everybody. He even sent some more business cards to the hotel. If I see someone of importance wandering around the corridors or sitting drinking by themselves, I will seize the moment, but I shall not seek.

'Hi, Tom.'

The voice is female and English. I turn sharply. It's Lizzy. She has a bottle of red lipstick on her face and a tight full-length black dress on.

'How's it all going, Lizzy? All set for tomorrow?'

'Fine. What are you doing tonight?' Lizzy doesn't hang about.

'Not much. I've been in Prague for a few days, so to be honest I was planning to hit the sack fairly early. I'm tired.' I even manage to yawn on cue.

'How about a drink? It'll be good fun.'

'Okay, but I must be in bed by eleven.'

'Don't worry, we will have you tucked up and enjoying your beauty sleep by eleven. See you here at seven then. Good. Ciao.'

With that she's gone. She has no need to stay. The deal has been struck. She struts off towards the lift. The tight-fitting dress draws in my eyes. The tighter a dress the more eyes it wants to accommodate.

*

Trepidation isn't my usual reaction to a drink with an elegant lady, but I am worried. Power is at the heart of all relationships whether those of work or pleasure. Lizzy is an attractive woman. I am made of flesh. Lizzy knows everyone here, I know virtually nobody. Lizzy could tempt me with promises. I should be ruthless, but all I feel is Radka-less.

Twelve hours ago I was in Radka's arms wishing for the moment to last for ever. Now I know why. I wanted time to stop because I didn't have tough choices to make, difficult paths to navigate, obstacles to avoid. I just had happiness, pure bliss.

I put on my jacket and look at my face in the mirror. The mirror shows an anxious face and a luxurious room. Bowls of fruit, pads of engraved paper, phones everywhere. The cost of the room must be astronomical. Fortunately, I am not paying the bill. It will all go on expenses. I am on a business trip. I should act like a businessman. The organiser of the event has invited me for a drink; I would be a fool to refuse.

Lizzy has slipped out of her dress and has put on a pair of jeans and a jumper. Her hair is tied back. Her lipstick has changed like a chameleon to match the colour of her mauve jumper. She sits and watches me approach. Around her sit her underlings. One, a short man with thick-framed glasses, is leaning over the arm of Lizzy's chair telling her a joke. Lizzy's face displays signs of interest in the anecdote, but she stares at me, not uttering a sound.

'Hello, Lizzy.' I announce my arrival to the assorted rabble.

Faces turn sharply. Some instantly recognise me and say 'Hi,' others just glare. Lizzy sits still, her eyelids kept continually apart by some bizarre magnetism. She puts down her drink, which she was clutching to her chest, and says mundanely, but loudly, 'Hi, Tom. Sit yourself down.'

'As I was saying,' the thick glasses continues not wanting my arrival to disrupt his progress, 'I think we should have a conference in Brazil soon.' He turns to look at me. Contempt is written all over his face. This is his moment and no one is going to spoil it.

Lizzy tuns back towards him, smiles, pats him on his knee and announces, again mundanely, again loudly, 'I think we should go. Tom has to be back by eleven.'

'Why?' asks a girl with a large nose.

'Because I need some sleep.'

'The conference starts tomorrow at nine. Have you no stamina? Have you got no energy? We're going to be out all night,' the short man announces. He looks round at everyone else, showing off his smug grin.

'Well, you'll have to forgive me. I am just a weak and feeble Englishman.'

Lizzy smiles. The glasses don't move. Lizzy leads her troops out of the lobby and on to the steps of the hotel. A cool gust of wind charges up the street and stings my face. I reach into my pocket and take out my black woollen hat. The other guests waiting on the steps of the hotel look at me with great displeasure. Expensive furs, jewellery, even the odd tiara are standing waiting for a taxi. How can they be waiting outside a hotel that admits a man wearing a pair of jeans, who has clearly failed to shave in the last twenty-four hours and is sporting a woollen black hat?

A taxi arrives and we jump in. I sit in the front. I do not want to tread on the thick glasses, who has been introduced as Tony. Lizzy shouts the name of the street to the taxi driver and then sinks back content to allow her admirers to entertain. Tony and William sit on either side of her. The anecdote competition continues.

I greet the driver in German. I start to engage him in a discussion on the weather. We talk the whole journey. I show no interest in the conversation of those behind me, only of him beside me. He waxes lyrical about the delights of Vienna. He points out various monuments. 'There behind you is the *Hofburg*.' I turn round. Lizzy looks straight at me, smiles, puts her index and third fingers to her face. They glide around. I smile back.

The taxi pulls up and the driver energetically describes how to get to the bar. We wander together as a group. Emily, the only female member of Lizzy's team, who has remained quiet throughout the journey, walks next to me.

'So, Tom, why were you in Prague? Were you interviewing somebody or something?'

Her question has a little too much probing for my liking.

'No, just on holiday, visiting an old friend.'

'What's it like? Prague, I mean, not your friend?'

'It's the most magical city on earth. When did you arrive in Vienna?'

'Day before yesterday.'

The conversation stops. We've exchanged the pleasantries, but neither of us have, at the moment at least, any inclination to continue the discussion. As Ed would say, we can't be arsed.

Lizzy, who is walking between Tony and William, turns her head and asks me matter-of-factly, 'So how was your little sojourn in Prague?' Her eyelids are raised as she says the word 'sojourn'.

'Wonderful. Thank you.'

'What did you do?' Her eyelids repeat their action on the word 'what'.

'I met a few old friends.'

'A few or', she pauses 'one in particular?'

I consider lying. I don't. 'If you really must know, Lizzy, my dear, I was visiting a beautiful Czech girl.' My eyelids are raised on the last word.

'Really. How delightful! You must be missing her already.'

I nod. It seems more genuine.

★

We wind up in a bar in the so-called Bermuda Triangle. I hope sincerely, however, I will not be lost for ever. The table is full of empty beer glasses. Time has ticked along. Eleven o'clock has been and gone. A man with ambition, a man with self-control wouldn't have allowed himself to be distracted by issues of the liver. Emily looks at me and smiles. She has barely touched any alcohol all evening. The conversation has deteriorated to the differences of male and female toilet habits. Lizzy, not someone whom I would imagine would talk of what she does in the confines of the little girls' room, cannot resist Tony and Will's provocative statements.

'So are you enjoying your stay in *Wien*.' I can't resist using the German.

'*Ja*,' replies Emily.

'Have you ever been to Vienna before?'

'I was in Vienna a couple of summers ago. It was wonderful.'

'Really?' My eyebrows rise. 'Couple of my friends were here then.'

'What are their names?'

'Ed, Clara and Mick.'

'Ed, Clara and Mick,' repeats Emily while her left hand travels up to her face. She gazes up at the ceiling. 'Ed, Clara and Mick. Um. I did meet someone called Ed, black hair about thirty, was a postman from Barking.'

I laugh as I try to picture Ed posting letters in Barking, whistling and talking in a Dick van Dyke cockney accent.

'No, that's not him.'

Emily looks at her watch.

'I'm going to head back. It's getting late.'

'I'll come with you.'

I get up. Emily puts on her coat. I put on mine. Tony and William's conversation is still somewhere in the toilet. Lizzy looks up at Emily and me.

'Where are you going?'

'Back to the hotel. I said I'd only have one drink.'

'And I said I would ensure you were tucked up by eleven. I am a woman of my word.'

With that announcement Lizzy rises from her seat, grabs her coat and my hand and pulls me towards the door.

The taxi ride back to the hotel drifts by. I have sunk too many pints, I've gone beyond my peak. Both Emily and Lizzy rest their heads on my shoulders. Both emit sighs. Both seem satisfied. The taxi driver looks at me through his rear-view mirror and winks.

We arrive back at the hotel. The lobby is full. All the armchairs are taken. Dinner jackets and bow ties are everywhere. An airline pilot, tall and uniformed, is checking in. The receptionist is repeating her welcome routine. She seems absorbed by the handsome face. She keeps giggling. 'If you are having any problems, please do not hesitate to call me.' She hands over the key, but doesn't let it go immediately. The pilot just smiles and gives the receptionist a little wink.

Emily excuses herself. She wants to check something in the main conference room, something about a sign. I walk to the lift with Lizzy. She has begun to talk about the conference. She seems tired already.

'Which floor?'

'Seven,' I reply.

'Good. Same as me.'

'What time are you getting up?' I ask, not too interested in the answer, just in passing the time of day.

'Half five,' she says, staring straight ahead at the lift doors waiting for them to open. 'You?'

'Eight.'

The doors open and Lizzy steps out.

'I've got something for you.'

We wander down to her room. Pictures of Vienna to the left and the right, soft padded carpet underfoot. She opens her door and in we go. She invites me to sit down. I perch on the end of the bed.

'Here,' she passes something to me, 'it's the conference programme. Have a look at it. I'll be back in a second.'

She goes into the bathroom. I can hear water rushing, gurgling, flushing. I'm too tired to take in the contents of the conference programme. I just lean back and rest my weary head against the wall.

The bathroom door closes. I feel a hand on my leg rubbing up and down. I raise my head. Lizzy is standing above me naked.

'Come on, Tom, let's see what you're made of.'

She starts to unzip my fly. Her hand reaches inside.

'Lizzy, Lizzy, Lizzy. Please Lizzy. Look Lizzy.'

'Look, It's just a bit of fun.'

She has undone my belt and has started to kiss my stomach.

'Please, Lizzy, I just... I've just been to Prague. I've just... I...'

She's started to undo my shirt buttons.

'Tom.' she sounds like a headmistress. 'Your little girl in Prague is never going to be told about this. It's just a bit of fun.'

I feel terrible. I am aroused. Lizzy is an expert after all. I want to think about Radka, but the flesh won't let me.

'I mean,' she continues, 'it's not as if she'd be too upset and try to end it all. She's probably at it anyway.'

Alcohol, exhaustion and Lizzy are too intoxicating. I give in.

THE CONFERENCE IS interesting I manage to collar a few characters and interview them. I distribute all my business cards. I even dine with a minor celebrity. My mind, however, is elsewhere, I've cracked the puzzle of Ed and Mick. The details are hazy, but the main thrust is clear. I want to return to London. I want to see Ed.

Time doesn't race, it strolls. Seconds take for ever. I keep pushing back my cuffs to look at my watch. Two, three, four o'clock. My plane doesn't leave for three hours, I keep scribbling in my notebook. I must seem to be industrious, but I just want to help the time along.

Periodically, I see Lizzy running from here to there, first a dignitary, then a hotel porter, then a photographer, then Emily running alongside her. Lizzy doesn't even acknowledge my existence. Emily, in contrast, offers me the occasional smile and the even more occasional 'Hi'. Tony and William are invisible. I heard a rumour they had been arrested for drunk and disorderly conduct. A malicious rumour, I'm sure.

ED HAS AGREED to meet up today. It is Sunday morning. I look out of my window. The sun has come out to enjoy its day. Chimneys, tiled roof and oblong windows fill the view. A jet-black crow perches on the next-door neighbour's wall. The smaller birds fly away.

I dress and walk quietly down the stairs so as not to wake everyone else. After a cup of tea and two slices of Marmite on toast, I put on my coat and wheel my cycle to the door. I hear footsteps coming down the stairs Emma is standing in her dressing gown.

'Where are you going?' she asks quizzically, as she runs both hands through her hair.

'I meeting Ed. We're going for a cycle.'

'It's not even nine on a Sunday morning. Are you mad? And what have you got in that envelope?' she asks, as she tightens the cord on her gown.

'I feel really energetic. Besides we have got a lot to talk about.' I motion towards the door.

'Tom, you haven't said anything about Prague or Vienna or anything since you got back.'

She sits down on the stairs, her feet pointing at my head. 'You haven't said anything about Radka or that Lizzy girl. What happened?'

'Prague, was, well, Prague was wonderful. Everything was great. Vienna was fun, in places.'

I'm not going to tell her which places. 'To be honest'. What a phrase that is. Anyone who uses that phrase has been waffling on about something, desperate to provide an explanation; then the waffler realises the explanation is not convincing the audience. so he prefixes the next plausible explanation with a 'to be honest'.

I continue, 'I'm shattered. Radka had me doing all sorts of things in Prague.'

Emma laughs. She's always the first to pick up on sexual innuendoes.

'And in Vienna, well, it was just non-stop.'

Emma laughs again. I'm just not up to speed.

'If you're so tired, why are you going cycling, so early?'

Emma may just have woken, may have had very little sleep, but her mind will always be sharper than mine. I shrug my shoulders and leave.

I cycle up the Walworth Road, weaving in and out of the red buses and cars. Drivers shout abuse, horns blare and lights turn from red to green with amazing regularity as pensioners, sticks raised in annoyance, cross the road. A delivery truck pulls up outside McDonald's and causes a minor jam. Drivers jump out of their cars and bawl, at the top of their voices, the panoply of English swear words. One driver seems to know them all, but is incapable of articulating any other word apart from 'you' which isn't vulgar. Two small children, walking hand in hand with their grandparents, stand and point at the mob. They are asking for an explanation. The adults seem reluctant to provide one.

I make my way up to Tower Bridge, dodging cars, motorbikes and tourists. Even in the depths of winter, there they are, cameras in hand, pointing at the bridge. The Japanese tourists nod constantly and politely ask the way, the Italians wander around in large groups and chatter, the Americans put their hands on their hips and just look.

Ed is already there. He has started to cycle every Sunday. It's his new routine; he goes to pray at the altar of fitness. Soon he will be confirmed in the faith, but he needs to see the priest a few more times. He stands tall and erect, his battered bike, the survivor of many journeys, leaning against the wall. He sees me approach and nods. We shake hands and exchange pleasantries.

I often feel strange after cycling. I feel refreshed. I feel fresh. I feel ready to face the trials and tribulations of the world. And yet I often feel my brain has stopped working, or is at least a little autonomous, not responding quickly and efficiently to my commands.

'Shall we cycle on?' asks Ed, as he grabs his water bottle and squeezes it sipping a thick, viscous, red liquid into his mouth. My mind starts to play around. Is he drinking blood or something? I've always thought he had long incisors.

'Sure. Let's go.'

We snake through Docklands. We pass converted warehouses on our left, the names of the old trading companies still visible above the second-floor bay windows. Where once products were hauled up and down, now stand balconies with overflowing pot plants. Onward we go. Onward past blocks of council houses with a variety of coloured doors, some red, some blue, some retaining their original wooden look.

We stop at a pub in the shadow of Canary Wharf. Its huge tower dwarfs everything in the vicinity. It stands as a landmark to the Eighties: big, brash and ultimately unsuccessful. Pointing to the sky, a light flickers from the top; down below everyone is caught in its shadow.

'So tell me about your journey to Bohemia,' Ed says, as he brings back two pints of Irish stout and a packet of salt and vinegar crisps. I rip open the packet, take a crisp, dunk it in the stout, place it carefully in my mouth and allow the vinegar to excite my tongue.

'It was great. Prague was wonderful; Vienna was business, but still fun.'

I look Ed in the eye, allow another crisp to slowly spread the sharp bite of vinegar all over my tongue, 'Ed,' I rub my nose, clear my throat and reach into my handlebar bag. There in among the puncture repair kit, my granddad's slightly rusted bicycle clip, and a spare battery for my rear light, is an envelope from my mother. I take it out, put my hand inside and take out two photographs. I place the two holiday snaps on Ed's side of the table and point at two things.

'I know, Ed. I know what went on on that journey, or at least I know the main thing that happened.'

Ed looks around. He seems to be searching for something, a hole in which to disappear or an eavesdropper, I don't know which, but he seems unnerved.

'Look. Can't we just leave it? If you know, you know. We don't have to have a trial, you know.'

I just look at Ed, a determined look is cast in stone. I point again at the pictures. I say nothing. We remain quiet for five minutes. I know because I'm counting silently.

Ed leans back on his chair, looks up at the sky and starts to speak. 'Two things fill the heart with ever renewed and increasing awe and reference, the more often and the more steadily we meditate upon them, the starry firmament above and the moral law within.' He turns his head towards mine and looks at me. His gaze is piercing. He seems to be reaching into my soul. 'I'll tell you the details because you've got the basic outline. I know you know, but I must make you swear to never ever tell anyone else.' I nod. 'Tom, say, "I promise".'

'I promise.'

'It all came to a head when we left you in Budapest. You were the lynchpin, you carried everyone on that journey. You were interpreter and guide. You were the bridge that joined us together. You were the one who kept us together, not allowing us to pull apart. Mick, big powerful Mick, man of steel, beer-swilling guzzler, well he was fine, fine that is until you left. I don't blame you for leaving, for going on to Prague. You met Radka after all.' Ed allows himself a smile as he mentions her name again. 'But, well, Mick probably had sublimated all his desires until you had left the scene.'

I am puzzled by Ed's choice of words. I know Ed loves to utilise the whole gamut of his extensive vocabulary, but is he about to slip from the sublime to the ridiculous?

'Mick had developed feelings of jealousy throughout the journey. That much was clear. He displayed his emotions on occasions, the sausage episode in St Petersburg being the prime example. He became increasingly convinced of some desire and he knew with you safety tucked away in a café in Budapest he could confront his desire.

'The journey to Vienna began well enough. Clara drank lots of Coke and engrossed herself in another Grisham, Mick gazed out of the window and I read the final chapters of *Anna Karenina*. Everything was fine until we crossed into Austria. We stopped unexpectedly at a seemingly insignificant station. I forget the name. A short man entered our compartment. He wore a blue suit and carried a leather briefcase with his initials, or what I assumed were his initials, embossed upon it. He greeted us and when he realised our nationality he began to engage us in conversation. Where had we been? Had we seen this? Had we done that? Clara and I were captivated by this small, bespectacled man. He talked and talked. His conversation traversed the whole terrain of conversation. He spoke about travel, the weather, the state of the railways and his child. All the while the train remained at the station; it refused to move on. Outside the guards wandered up and down. Other passengers were gazing out of their compartment windows, hoping to find an explanation blowing in the wind.

'Mick became increasingly agitated. He had, if you remember, planned this part of the journey. The train was scheduled to arrive in Paris at eight o'clock the next morning. He had decided to take a train out of Paris two hours later. Seconds ticked away. A prompt arrival appeared more and more elusive. He began to pace up and down the compartment and then along the carriage corridor. He even stepped off the train on to the platform and began to ask the train official why there was a delay. The ticket inspector's knowledge of English was, however, about as extensive as Mick's knowledge of German. Baffled looks. Shoulders shrugged. He stared through our compartment window. Clara, myself and the Austrian gentleman, Erich, were laughing. Clara was recounting the story of the bread shop in Tallinn. Happiness was on one side of the window, unhappiness on the other.

'Eventually, we began to move. Mick kept eyeing his watch. He was desperate to catch that train. "If I were you," said Erich looking at Mick, "I would sit down and relax. There is nothing you can do about the speed of the train. It's one of those things we have no control over. The train will arrive in Paris when the train arrives. The most important thing is to enjoy your time during the journey. We aren't hastening the end, but the end will come sooner for us."

'We pulled into another small station and Erich got off. "I will ring my wife from here. It is not too far from here," he announced, as he took his bag and coat. "Lovely chap," said Clara. "Yeah, really interesting," I said. "Fascinating," said Mick, his voice laced with venomous sarcasm. The train eventually left the station and continued its crawl. Clara excused herself and went to the toilet. "I think you're going to be unlucky and miss the connection in Paris," I said. Mick narrowed his eyes and reached into his pocket and…' Ed stopped, took one of the crisps, took a sip of beer and leant back. 'Well, you know the rest. I've filled in the details.'

'Come on, Ed, you've got to finish,' I say desperate to hear the end.

'But you know it. So why should I tell you a story you already know?' asks Ed, jutting his chin forward and feeling his stubble with his left hand.

'Ed, I know what he did, but I don't know why.'

'He was a jealous man, probably still is. He wants things for himself and for no one else to have even a sniff, even a platonic sniff. He, well, he put his hand into his pocket and…'

Ed starts to rub his wrists and then his hands, as if he is washing them, washing off the dirt, cleansing them. His voice becomes quieter and deeper. 'Then, it all happened so quickly. Then he lunged at me with a knife. "I've fucking had it with you. Are you going to tell me what's been going on?" he screamed. "I've seen the way you've been looking at Clara. Well, she's mine, all fucking mine." "Look, Mick, Mick." I said. My voice was surprisingly quiet and calm. I was just stunned. It's not every day someone puts a huge blade in one's face. "I haven't done anything. Look, she's your girlfriend, I wouldn't touch her." He fell on his knees and started to weep. Then he started to rub his knife against his wrists; blood began to drip on to the floor. I fell on my knees and pleaded with him to stop. He dropped his knife, put both hands to his face and sobbed and sobbed. He looked a sad, pathetic sight.

'I didn't know what to do. I took out of my bag a half-used toilet roll. I wrapped what tissue I had around his wrists and then began to mop up the floor. He rubbed his red eyes and blew his nose. I reached up and took down my bag from the luggage rack and rummaged through my belongings until I found my old tennis sweatbands. The ones you can see', he points at the photograph, so proudly displayed on Mum's mantlepiece, taken on a beach in France, 'on Mick's wrists.'

'Why didn't you tell me?' I enquire.

'Because I promised Mick. He told me he would kill me if I told anyone else. And judging by his behaviour on that train journey, I wasn't going to take any chances. Besides, I am a man who keeps his promises.'

We cycle back at a leisurely pace. The rain begins to fall, but it doesn't matter. We don't mind getting wet.